McDaid's Wife

Acknowledgements

Extract from *Krapp's Last Tape* by Samuel Beckett quoted by kind permission of Faber & Faber Ltd., London, and Grove Press Inc., New York.

Extract from *Collected Poems* by W.H. Auden (Poem V from 'Twelve Songs') quoted by kind permission of Faber & Faber Ltd., London, and Random House Inc., New York.

McDaid's Wife

a novel by

Jill Anders

Marion Boyars
London · New York

Published in Great Britain and the United States in 1988
by Marion Boyars Publishers
24 Lacy Road, London SW15 1NL
26 East 33rd Street, New York, NY 10016

Distributed in the United States by
Kampmann & Co., Inc., New York

Distributed in Canada by
Book Center Inc., Montreal

Distributed in Australia by
Wild & Woolley Pty Ltd., Glebe, N.S.W.

© Jill Anders 1988

British Library Cataloguing in Publication Data

Anders, Jill
    McDaid's wife: a novel. — (Iris series).
    I. Title   II. Series
    823'.914 [F]   PR6051.N3/

Library of Congress Cataloging in Publication Data

Anders, Jill, 1930–
    McDaid's wife.

    (Iris series)
    I. Title.   II. Series.
    PR6051.N37M3   1988   823'.914   87–21052

ISBN 0-7145-2881-1

Typeset by Ann Buchan (Typesetters) in 12/14pt Baskerville and Souvenir
Printed and bound in Great Britain by
Biddles Ltd, Guildford and King's Lynn

Schlachtensee

William McDaid sat on a hill overlooking lake
Schlachtensee, taking long pulls on his cigarette.

There was a combination of repose and tension about
him which gave the effect of absolute calm. This was
deceptive, his blood was in such ferment he could feel the
pounding of his heart.

From his position on the hill, the lake seemed divided
into two parts. The surface of the water shone blue-black.
Drops flashed off the oars of a long boat. Childrens' voices
were mixed with birdsong, there was a splash and a shout
from a swimmer below as strollers talked beside the lake
edge.

He had never experienced such sharpness of detail,
never heard sounds so clearly or beheld such colours. He
found the acuteness of his senses almost painful.

In the palm of his hand lay a gold fish pendant on a chain.

"Anneliese," he murmured.

Susurration of leaves, of grasses.

"Anneliese."

The name was taken up by the breeze, touched the water and was fixed by the sun.

He lay on his back in the pine needles with eyes closed and mouth open, ravished by his senses.

A Dream of War

Tessa McDaid had dreams of great clarity where she was no longer the victim of circumstance and had gained a certain control over events. The same, however, could not be said about her life. Dreams pursued her from South Africa to England, from Ireland to Spain to West Berlin where, curled up in a solid oak bed beside her husband, William, she dreamt again.

She had begun the long walk home over the hills when suddenly she changed her mind, deciding to take the train instead. On the way to the station she saw a fighter plane swoop down over the horizon, heard the distant rattle of machine-gun fire and realized the country was at war.

Quickly she made for the old warehouses through which she had to pass in order to reach the platform. In the first warehouse people lay in rows on the floor. An instructor stood over them: a tall man with a long meditative face and mandarin beard. She was forced to lie down also.

"This is called The Dark," he said, "these are black searchlights. When they are directed at you your minds will go black, and it is only I who can snap you out of it." Terrified, she began to worm her way back towards the door when she was transfixed by a black beam which plunged her into impenetrable darkness. There she lay rigid with terror, when suddenly, with a click of his fingers, she was released.

"The next test," he said quietly, "is done with sound. Certain sounds have been recorded which try the mind beyond endurance. I doubt whether any of you will survive. This is the culmination of years of research, the most severe of all tests." Voices began gabbling, interrupted at regular intervals by the sound of a bell. The bell became intolerable, the voices insinuated themselves into the inner convolutions of her brain and rose to a pitch. To counteract this mounting pressure she began reciting nursery rhymes to herself. "Three blind mice. . ."

"Do I see your lips moving?" He was standing over her.

"No," she said.

"You have all done very well," he announced finally with a sigh. "Now you must learn to throw stones. These warehouses have to be destroyed within a week."

As he spoke a collection of dolts appeared from nowhere and, laughing uproariously, proceeded to hurl enormous rocks at the pillars and crossbeams which supported the roof. As the steel rang under the assault, and the structure began to totter and collapse, she rose from the floor and ran out to the station platform.

Then she was on a country path with the instructor coming towards her wrapped in his own thoughts.

"One of the lonely ones," he muttered to himself as she passed.

Tessa opened her eyes to the dawn light. Her husband slept quietly beside her. Getting out of bed, she tip-toed across the black-painted floor to the wooden-railed balcony and looked down at the garden. The lawn, cherry tree, lilac bush, apple trees, black currant bushes were bathed in a peaceful green light, the air was still, the birds sang, the morning sun had struck the tops of the pine trees. It was the start of a regular Berlin summer's day. The house like a ship travelling through a green land, with her at the prow.

It was feasible to dream of war, she reasoned to herself. Although the garden itself was peaceful, the larger picture was not. The Russians had encircled West Berlin which was occupied by British, French and American forces, and the great food trains which rumbled through Nicolassee had crossed the bleak territory of the Russian zone.

Nature was powerless, mute against the grasping hand of the superpowers.

She felt pleased to own no house, no land, that she had no such claims; pleased that her family was all her life.

Then, as she gazed down at her sleeping husband, she fancied for a moment that she saw there the face of the instructor. Why? They did not resemble each other in the least, the dream man had authority, was blonde to the point of being ethereal, frail in spite of his height, with a languid abstracted air, while William who was dark and crafty, lay like a dozing leprechaun, an eyelid away from trouble. He was no instructor. She smiled to herself and went downstairs, putting the thought out of her mind.

Beethoven's Fifth

"That day you arrived, I remember it," said
Rosalinde Hindemann, lighting a candle in an old pewter
candlestick and setting it against the window. She and her
husband Walter lived in a house so heavily eaved it
seemed to sink into the ground. Turning to her guests,
Tessa and William McDaid, she said, almost breath-
lessly:

"You came like refugees."

She was a large, sensual woman with a touch of the
gipsy about her, dark defiant eyes, the skin below tinged
with blue.

A poker light suspended from the low ceiling lit up the
drawing room obliquely — shelves of books in the corner,
her own pottery, a basket of needlework open, childrens'
clothes drying on a chair.

"So you did," agreed Walter, .

"*Ja*, each with a bag, walking up the path. Now the smell of roast meat comes from the kitchen!" She gave an earthy laugh.

"You must know by now that you are amongst the élite, here in Nicolassee," Walter remarked, adjusting his trousers which were prone to sink to the hips. His shirt, too, seemed to be made for a much larger man. He had over-exposed features, an avid look in the eye, a long narrow nose, high cheekbones, wispy hair and a receding hairline. A face, once handsome, now worn with damaged hopes and flushed with booze. With trembling hands he uncorked the wine, pouring it into thick green glasses. "Surely you have heard the Trüters whistle for their children from the front gate, the opening bars of Beethoven's Fifth? Ah, that is culture. We are very cultivated here in Nicolassee." His lip curled.

"That detail has escaped me," said William.

William McDaid, who was Irish, had a hardiness and sharpness about him. In sleep he may have resembled a leprechaun, but awake he had a face of such rigidity you could play handball against the planes of his cheeks. He had the dark stare of a nocturnal animal, a sharp foxy nose and a pointed, well-trimmed beard.

Standing his lighted cigarette on the table on its filter, he remarked:

"What I marvel at is the providence of the Teutonic mind. Take our neighbour's garden: those logs already stacked at the foot of the pine tree for winter, not one out of place, a minor masterpiece, and could it be their white tree is fed on milk?"

"Bourgeois preoccupations," growled Walter.

Tessa McDaid, sunk in an armchair, her long legs crossed, watched the antics of her husband with a dangerously unreserved affection. She was a tall South African with high-arched eyebrows and green eyes, a cross between a beauty and a clown, natural and spontaneous, with lapses into reflection and brooding.

"What surprises me about Berlin," she said in her soft drawl, "is the freshness of the climate, this wash of air as if clothes were superfluous."

"So they are," purred Walter, his lascivious eyes on her legs. "How nice," he said, shining down on her with affection. "How very nice to hear the English language again, and so beautifully spoken. For me there is no language like it in the world. And, may I say," he said turning to William, "to have an Irish author in the house, that is a great pleasure. William is very gifted," he said to Rosalinde. "A very talented fellow."

"I can see it in his eyes," she said, giving William a wink.

"A young and talented writer. I return your article, William," he said, placing an issue of *The Dublin Magazine* on the table. "I read it with much pleasure. You have the world before you already." He leaned over the table at this point and looked at him curiously. "I saw you on the banks of the Schlachtensee the other day, staring at something as if you would split it in two. Was it a stone?"

William coloured slightly. "Gawking's a national pastime with us," he said.

"Take a warning from Socrates," said his host, "concentrating on something like that with all your senses you could lose your mind."

"Never fear, it's ingrained. We Irish are like that, riveted by nature. I recall a man in a Dublin pub murmuring over his pint: 'Ah, the hawthorn! The hawthorn!' "

"Horton? What's that?" asked Rosalinde.

Walter had a pedantic manner with her, as if he dealt with a complete barbarian. "*Der Hagedorn.*"

"Are you a novelist?" Rosalinde asked.

"I take a long look at Irish writing; the writer against the landscape," said William, rolling up *The Dublin Magazine* into a telescope, placing one end to his eye and veering it at the window. "Yes, I see him now, sitting peacefully in the rain on an old copy of *The Irish Times*, soaked with words."

Rosalinde who had followed his gaze into the garden realized he was clowning and laughed till her breasts trembled.

"Very funny," she said.

Putting the magazine down William became serious.

"When we buried my mother in Glasnevin Cemetery my father remarked: 'Tis a strange cold wind blows here summer and winter.' Poets all," he announced, draining his glass.

Tess, who preferred to sit back and watch rather than participate, listened to William and marvelled how she could ever have married him for his silences. She was uncommonly static in company and although her body was disposed in an attitude of rapt attention she was not listening.

Looking at their reflections in the window, she wondered whether they too concealed this other person of whom they could not speak, who bore their sadness and fears while they laughed and lifted their glasses. Walter had been in the SS. Was there some guilt he could not confess, even to his wife? Perhaps, yes. He was like a penitent, his eyes too polished, with an innocence no one might read. And then he kept so clean and smelled of soap. And Rosalinde, so sure in all her ways, what did she hide? A child of the war who ran barefoot through the rubble, eating her fists? What depths had hunger driven her to? One never knew. And as to William, who above all concealed someone else, she thought she saw him quite clearly: a conjuror who revealed a box within a box within a box, the sleight of hand never ceased and tears she had never seen flowed from his eyes. After a while she surfaced.

"Last night I dreamt of war," she said. "There was an interrogator."

"Funny you should dream that," remarked Walter, "did you know the Nazi Headquarters for Military Intelligence were here in Nicolassee? Here, twenty years ago?"

"No!"

"And even yesterday there were troop movements. You'd think the war had never ended."

"Troop movements? Where?"

"Along Potsdamer Chaussee."

"Which troops?"

"The Americans."

"A military exercise?"

"A display of force. Something has aroused the Russians again. They tighten the noose and the Yanks retaliate. Once more we feel cut off from the world." He sighed.

"And the gunfire from the Teltower Canal, did you hear it?" asked Rosalinde.

"I heard something," said William.

"Some poor devil was shot by the Russians, trying to swim across."

"The Russians are bad enough but the Yanks are not my favourite people either," Walter said. "You once asked me about the last days of the war, William. I wasn't in the mood to tell it then. A time of general panic, of course. Myself and a friend tried to walk back home across Germany. We came to a large hill and suddenly found ourselves looking down at the Autobahn. Below us the American troop convoys were moving eastwards. Terrified, we flattened ourselves on the hilltop, concealed, or so we thought, by the long grass. But we were caught and put into an American camp." He had a soft expressive mouth, so mobile he appeared to smile as he spoke. "I was sixteen.

We ate American chocolate, there was nothing else. We stood around in the rain. When the sun came out the mud hung from our overcoats like lumps of dried dung. These knocked together as we walked, producing a bell-like sound, like cattle in a field."

"Oh, you and the war!" protested Rosalinde, "When do I hear the end of that?" She turned to William. "You look smart. What is that you wear?"

"This," he said, puffing out his chest, "is a kind of waistcoat, after Hemingway. My good wife made it."

"I copied it from a photograph," said Tess.

"You are clever," Rosalinde said in admiration, "and you've three beautiful sons. I like them to eat here in my house. To see children eating together makes me very happy."

Despite Rosalinde's dark moods, which were there in the shadows of her face, Tess found her irresistible. She accepted the most strenuous tasks with good grace, with her powerful arms she kept the old coal furnace for the central heating going in the basement. On their small income she had mastered the details of living to a point worthy of celebration. Home was the centre of the universe where laughter and children could thrive. Not for her the Sèvres vase, the objets d'art; things grew beautiful with necessity, clothes lying about waiting to be ironed were a decoration in themselves, the reclining shirt an invitation. Good smells, too, were part of this ethos: clean towels drying, the goulash at that moment cooking in the oven for dinner. No one is satisfied, however, and she wanted her own pottery. But she would have that too, she had ordered a second-hand potter's wheel.

Rosalinde, for her part, was attracted to Tess. She admired her lissomeness, her easy ways, and she had trusted her from the start. A private person like that, she knew, kept confidences. She also judged mothers by their children and liked the vitality of the McDaid boys who gambolled like cubs in her garden.

"I saw you on the Rehwiese, Tess, on your new bicycle, with Jonathan at the back. You went so fast round the curves I thought he would fall off, but he was laughing. You take chances."

"The mother will never grow up," said William.

"You were singing too, what were you singing?"

"Oh, things to amuse," Tess said. "*Kalamazoo* — I've got a girl. . ."

"Talking about Jonathan," Walter said, gazing out of the window at the lamplight shafting through the trees onto the motionless swing and the sandpit, "Yesterday I looked out and saw him there. Funny, the garden seemed full of children, and yet he was alone."

"You have a good home for the children," said Rosalinde, "better than this. I saw your landlady, Frau Weidner, coming out of the house yesterday. What is she doing here?"

"It's part of the lease," explained Tess, "that she comes to stay for a couple of days each month. She leaves tomorrow."

"Aha," laughed Rosalinde. "Keeping an eye on you, clever old bitch!"

"We don't mind, she's unobtrusive, helps with the babysitting, after all."

"She's so correct."

"Yes, correct, God help us."

"Where does she sleep?"

"Up in the attic. She has a room of her own."

"She and the dog? Have you been in there?"

"No."

"The mind boggles at the secret life of Frau Weidner." Remarked William.

"So," said Rosalinde, "D.A.A.D. provides the house and Frau Weidner collects the money."

"And we have a year of grace," said Tess, "and high living."

"D.A.A.D. is a bit of a mystery to us," said William, "What do you think of it?"

"A curious phenomenon the *Deutscher Akademischer Austausch Dienst*," Walter admitted, "Quite phoney, of course, politically based. Artists like yourselves from the so-called Free World are invited here for a year or so as a showcase to Communist Europe. The way this government thinks appals me. Don't misunderstand, I applaud the idea in principle, but not as political strategy, which it is. The Director of D.A.A.D., for instance, has his foot on the ladder. It's a key position."

"They're an incongruous bunch," said Tess, "all conforming to type. The British shabby and plausible, the

Greeks wily, the Americans expansive, Italians volatile, and the Irish, well. . ."

"Maggoty," put in William. "Receptions are held where we misbehave and scowl across the room. The Japanese composer is the exception, perched inflexibly with his little knees clenched tightly together, smiling. The smell of achievement is odious."

"And yet," said Tess, "I suspect that most of us emerge from semi-poverty and will return to it once the dream is over."

"Well, you must enjoy yourselves," said Walter, filling up the glasses.

"I will show you the charms of Charlottenburg. There we will drink raspberry beer."

"Ach, you and Charlottenburg," pouted Rosalinde.

"I have an old friend in Charlottenburg," Walter said dreamily.

"A fancy woman, you mean," retorted his wife.

"I must see her again soon."

"He gets this red eye," she said, "then he goes to Charlottenburg. How boring it is."

Tess noticed that a half moon had appeared in the upper part of the window, lying on its back. It pleased her to think she was facing south.

"All your friends," carped Rosalinde, "are from University days. They have made something of their lives. They come here to see you and what do they see? The eternal student, still dreaming."

Walter laughed. "I remind them of the good times."

"Rubbish!"

Tess, who had begun to tire of Rosalinde's nagging mood, gave her attention to the window. She had discovered that, due to a fault in the glass, the moon could become liquid, changing shape from crescent to saucer to globule of light if she lowered her head, and that she could reverse the process, oozing it slowly up into its crescent form again.

Nicolassee

"We keep young with gold and silver pills, you know," said Frau Weidner referring to her friends in Wiesbaden, "Gold for the men and silver for the women. They give us a passion for life. You know what I mean?"

Twinkling her blue eyes, she smiled suggestively.

The ancient capers in Wiesbaden should be quite something, Tess thought, returning the smile.

Before departing Frau Weidner was giving her dog its morning ablutions on the patio. She was a small woman with dyed-blonde hair and speckled hands.

"*Ach doch*, Tutti," she clucked, wiping its eyes with a cotton bud. "*Bist doch ein guter Hund!* Sometimes I leave Tutti with Max and his wife, friends outside Wiesbaden. They love dogs but they do not have one for themselves, no, not after the last one died. Max was so sad, he kept the skin and sewed it up, putting some cotton wool inside, but it's not the same. The body is like a *Schlange*, how do you call it?"

"A snake?"

"*Ja*, and the face pointed like a fox. No, definitely not the same." She took a small brush out of a bag and passed it over the animal's trembling haunches. "Still, Max, he sleeps with it every night."

Once Frau Weidner had left for Wiesbaden, Tess went up to the attic. The place attracted her: the shape of the roof, its crossed rafters, heady smell of pine, the silent and brooding quality of objects collected over a lifetime. Open slatted shelves reached from floor to ceiling stacked with the old lady's possessions: vases, crockery, silver, an old clock, lacquered trays, linen, towels and blankets meticulously folded in piles, books, old journals and newspapers.

Seating herself on the floor with her bare feet crossed in front of her, she began to flip through a pile of old magazines. Perspiration formed at the nape of her neck from heat and curiosity, running down her back in cold beads.

Distantly she could hear the children calling to each other in the garden and from the study below came the tap-tap of William's typewriter, the little engine that carried them all along.

Amongst the magazines, now faded and sepia-coloured, she came upon the Olympic Issue of *Die Berliner*

Illustrierte Zeitung, August 1936, price 1 mark, a collector's piece. The cover in pastels which featured the crowning of the Aryan champion with a laurel wreath, had predictable political overtones and on the first page Adolf Hitler descended the stairs of the Olympic Stadium, dressed austerely and sporting only one medal, his right hand bent back in acknowledgment of the crowd's applause. He was flanked by members of the Olympic Committee and a posse of eagle-eyed henchmen looking for trouble. The clock on the stadium tower registered twelve o'clock exactly and his moustache, like a postage stamp, registered twelve noon also. No smile, of course, that familiar seething look. Germany had won the Games with 33 gold medals, a tremendous achievement, but could it have been otherwise?

Frau Weidner would have been in her early thirties then, how did she judge the war now, widowed as a consequence of that national euphoria, munching her way through a plethora of cream cakes into the German post-war miracle? Hard to tell, she never spoke of it, and appeared to survive unscathed. Unlike the one-legged veteran Tess had seen in the park whose empty trouser leg was tucked up with a safety pin, and whose yellow armband, emblazoned with three black spots, indicated he was blind also. Dark glasses hiding his sightless eyes, he smiled as he sat there each day in the golden palace of the sun.

"If I were in East Berlin now, with my brother, the police would hit me over my bald head," he had once confided to William. Tess, however, had not spoken to him until one particular day. The time having come for him to leave, he put on his hat as usual, reached around for his crutches and levered himself up in one smart movement, pivoted round to face the path he could not see and proceeded on his way. But this time, much to her alarm, he soon lost direction and veered towards a tree, each massive lurch bringing him closer until, within seconds, he had struck it with terrible force. He did not fall, however, neither did he make any sound or call for help.

She left the children and rushed across the forbidden grass, returned the fallen crutch to his hand, picked up the hat and placed it on his head, when she noticed blood coursing down his forehead. "*Danke schön! Danke schön!*" he said brightly, indicating he wanted no fuss.

With that he poled off slowly, then he halted and still looking ahead called back to her: "Are the children with you?"

"Yes." How on earth did he know about them?

Nodding approval he proceeded down the path, zig-zagging from edge to edge, his shoulders out like two great wings, face covered in blood, an angel of misfortune. The war widows, sitting on their benches with mouths agape, had not moved a muscle. People did not connect, they were isolated from each other. By what?

Tap-tap went the typewriter below. She rose and put the magazines away, except for the Olympic issue, which she tucked under her arm. As she went down beneath the stained glass window, running the bannister under her hand, she decided that pale green was the colour unique to Berlin. She would write to her mother about that pale green light which filtered into the house from the garden and bathed the sky at times. She would tell her too about new sensations, smells of the earth, appetizing flavours: the wines, the cheeses, the bread, apfelsaft and the pastry shop on the corner.

In the sitting-room her youngest son, Jonathan, played the Memory Game alone on the floor. The cards were made in pairs, you put them face down and turned up two at a time, the one with the most pairs won. He was doing this with uncanny speed; at two years old the family champion.

She watched him, wondering if this tenacity would last. Who were they? What were they? One day it would be easy to say of her children "I saw that from the beginning", but now? Impossible. An exhibition of drawings by Sam glowed against the plate glass windows of the conservatory: clowns and birds drawn with felt pens, illuminated by the sun gave the effect of stained glass. They were talented and affectionate. Funny too, particularly Nicholas. She remembered his remark when they watched Buñuel's *Robinson Crusoe* on television: finding some corn, Crusoe made a field, sowed the grains and in an old trunk, found a girl's dress to drape a scarecrow. On leaving the field he glanced back to see the wind had filled it out, giving the dress body, a girlish shape. A poignant expression passed over Crusoe's face as he went back to take the fabric in his hands. The suggestion was highly romantic, but Nicholas had seen something else. He looked up at her with his eyes alight.

"*I* know," he said, "it reminds Robinson Crusoe of his mother."

Tessa McDaid was not a woman of the southern hemisphere for nothing. She liked to walk barefoot in summer, feel the texture of the grass beneath her feet, the stone flags on the patio, the wooden floorboards and carpets of the house. She had long slender feet and her hands, too, were long and slim. She liked to wear close-fitting trousers cut off to just below the knee, her shirt open to the third button, her hair in two bunches like a girl, or caught up in a high ponytail, with tendrils falling about her face. She got very brown, felt at home in the unrestricting clothes of summer, was conscious of light and shade on the skin.

No paragon of wifely virtues she did, however, put a few drops of lavender in the rinsing water of the family wash so that the clothes and sheets were faintly perfumed. She made fruit drinks with ice, flavoured with mint, prepared pineapples, slicing off the peel and retaining the stem, to freeze like that, ready to slice.

They ate all their meals on the patio. Large bowls of mixed salad: lettuce, tomato, cucumber, radish, celery, green and red peppers, carrots cut fine, watercress, avocado pear, slices of apple – many colours of red and green tumbled together in a rich dressing — crisp and fresh to taste. This she served with cheeses and brown bread, followed by a bowl of cherries from the garden.

Delphiniums and marguerites were arranged in vases throughout the house, the windows opened first thing in the morning to let in the pine-forest air. The garden waved its little flags: breezes heavy with scents vibrated the foliage, the grasses, leaving the blackcurrant bushes trembling like wire.

Barefoot and easy, she enjoyed her children, made daisy chains for them, whistles out of blades of grass stretched between her thumbs. She liked to roll on the lawn with them in her arms, feel their supple bodies against her. They were healthy, their eyes bright. "Look at me!" they pleaded for approbation, climbing trees, standing on their heads, walking on the wall, hanging out of windows, calling from the balcony "Look! Look!"

But she had a vivid interior life of her own, nourished by reading. In a way things were played out in front of her as if she were a witness to an unfolding drama, the meaning of which she had not yet grasped, but she knew that she saw more than most people and her vision was not commonplace. She had an ironic view of the world.

Nicolas, hiding in the long grass, would rise up suddenly, bitten by an ant, while the birds sang.

William mowed the lawn and, as if the scents were not enough, there came the added aroma of the sweet cut grass. He would take the deck-chair out in the shade and settle down with a book. Jonathan, standing by to light his cigarette, loved to strike the match.

Sometimes they would set off on their bicycles, Jonathan perched behind his mother, Nicolas and Sam following, along the bicycle lanes, smelling the gardens as they passed, to collect swans' feathers from the Wannsee and bathe.

Sometimes she thought: this is the time you will remember as best, grasp it with all your senses.

Now, as she descended the stairs from the attic, Tess became aware that the typing had stopped and immediately had a sense of unease. William had become enigmatic, would pause before answering a question and then reply evasively. She was nervous of talking to him. Once they had interpreted each other's dreams, now she was left with silences. These silences had a certain power over her, as did the fact that she neither knew nor asked what he wrote. She decided to go up one day soon, when he was out, and see for herself.

She was half aware of the voice of the serpent which whispers, when all is well, all will not be well, for it was at times like these that William would bolt, thinking his absence unnoticed, unaware he was the pivot round which all revolved, or that the things Tess did were done first of all for him.

Sam, who had the ability to remain still for a long time once his attention was fixed, lay in the grass, absorbed by the antics of the red squirrels. Pursuing each other relentlessly in the pines, their sharp claws nicking into the russet bark, they paused, splayed out, pulsating against the trunk with their eyes rolling, before spiralling off once again.

He also had one eye on the kitchen door and saw Tess emerge. She comes out at last, he thought to himself, is she looking for me? No. Lies down on the lawn. What about lunch? Last night I dreamt I ate the moon.

Once again William had disappeared without a word. A note from him lay on the hall dresser: 'Gone out for a drink'. His furtiveness drove her to distraction. She crumpled it up angrily and threw it in the drawer, went up to the study, sat down and switched on the desk light. Heavy with guilt, she opened his diary and feverishly turned the pages looking for her name, apprehensive of what she might find. Although there was a page for each day the entries were sparse, now and again the symbol for sex between them. Her name did not appear.

"So that is all I count for," she thought bitterly. The writing was minute, purposely illegible perhaps. There were random comments. "Brain coddled" or was it "curdled"? "Beware the great soporific." "I cannot be abused enough. Thrive on that. Mind as cold as ice." And then "Die here before the page." "Remember Gatto-pardo. Light at the end of the tunnel?"

There was no recent work in sight: all the indications of writer's block. The typing she had heard must have been correspondence. She closed the diary and went downstairs, troubled.

A house may appear serene enough, she thought, but its rooms can become uneasy chambers of the mind.

"I left my diary marked at a certain page," said William, lolling drunkenly against the door jamb. "Now I find the marker has been moved. It is not written for you to understand. You are *intruding!* Leave me alone! I came to Berlin to get away from you. You could have stayed in Spain. Why did you come?"

Tess ignored the abuse. "We belong together," she said, "and the children need a proper education."

"Education, pah! Nicolas and Sam find themselves in a German Gymnasium, they are at a full stop, unable to understand or speak a word. Nicholas was attacked at school. Have you forgotten what he said: 'They hate me and I begin to hate myself'?"

"As you know D.A.A.D. has promised them a place in the Kennedy School. I must admit I'm disappointed it's taking so long. What's the matter with you anyway?"

He stood swaying in the doorway, then lurched forward and sat down putting his head in his hands. Presently he said: "I'm hoping for something new to happen, looking for it."

"Like what?"

He looked up at her through his fingers marvelling how obtuse she was. "Nothing explicit," he said, after a while.

"Where do you drink? Who do you drink with? Where do you go?"

He lit a cigarette, hoping that, if he waited long enough, the question would dissolve in mid-air like the smoke. The silence became a scream to her.

"Where-do-you-go?" she repeated slowly. "*Answer me!*"

"No say," he said finally, slipping out of the room.

Leviathan

The McDaids had hit calm weather again, but not for long

In the bath William soaped himself with his hands, shampooed his hair and beard and lay back smiling with his head submerged.

"My God, Mr Pisces," said Tess, arranging her long hair in front of the mirror. "You're in your element."

William rose like Pan from the bath. The thick dark matted hair which circled his nipples etched a broad line from umbilicus to groin where growth was fierce, thinning only at the shanks which curved in an arc away from the knee. A neat pair of hooves would not have been out of place.

What sort of a man was he apart from looking like

a goat? His lapsed catholicism was a help, his faint conscience appeased by the idea of the confessional and the absolution of blame. He longed for a telegram, source unspecified, where all was forgiven. But he had moments of self criticism:

"You are all my trouble," he said sternly, staring down at his member, blind worm which foraged in primeval fuzz.

In search of a safety pin to hold up her skirt, Tess switched on the desk light in William's study, and was taken aback to find before her on the blotter a gold fish pendant on a chain. What was this? A gift to William? From whom? The bauble glinted at her like the sun off the brass trumpets surrounding Jericho. With instant clarity she saw the fortress of her family come tumbling down. In a moment she had picked it up and hurled it out into the garden thinking, "Such love as winds you round casts me *out*!", went up to the window and saw the plants stir a little, that was all. Once she had done this she felt an irrational sense of calm restored and put the incident to the back of her mind.

"These foolish things
    remind me of you-o-o-o-!"
warbled William as he dressed.

They were off to dine in Tegel with Laura Aventura, a Spanish poetess and Anglophile whom they had met on their arrival in Berlin. Laura found William amusing and liked the seriousness of Tess. She was middle-aged and worldly, a woman of spirit who lived alone.

In the Underground neither spoke, while the ravaged face of the actor Martin Held gazed down at them from a playbill advertising Samuel Beckett's *Krapp's Last Tape* at the Schiller Theater. They had both seen it. Tess thought of the actor preparing himself for the part. Wearing that rusty black waistcoat and trousers, collarless white shirt open to the navel, he could be moving towards the dressing-room mirror to apply greasepaint beneath his eyes. Then she began to watch William's reflection in the glass as she sometimes watched the clock, passively waiting for the hour to strike.

Had he missed it? Had he missed the pendant?

Having at last reached Laura's address they rang the bell at the garden gate and were addressed by the gatepost in her rich contralto "I'll be down!" At last she appeared, a small round priestess in a loose-fitting robe. "Keys! Keys!" she puffed as they went up the stairs. "What a nuisance! One for the gate, another for the front door, another for the bottom of the stairs, and one for my apartment. Four altogether. What a country! Can you believe it? Am I besieged, can you tell me, or am I merely my own prisoner?" She looked up at them and smiled. "But at last I have a place of my own and you are my first guests. As we say: *Mi casa es su casa.*"

35

The long room was on two levels, a table and chairs stood in the bay window, red and rigid, the table laid for three gleaming in the evening sun. "I painted that furniture myself, finished only yesterday and now quite beautiful, don't you think?"

"Indubitably," remarked William, dismayed there was no comfortable chair in the room.

Tess felt overwhelmed by Laura, as if she were held under the pulsating breast of some large bird. The place surprised her. To one side stood a screen with poems pinned onto the silk: "The red and green kingfishers flash between the orchids and clover, one bird casts its gleam on another," one read. A large erotic poster on the wall featured Japanese love-making. Two figures in ceremonial dress lay, one over the other, fluid flowing from their nether regions like a shoal of minnows. One image upon another served to disturb her, and she thought of Beckett's play:

> ". . . the eyes just slits, because of the glare, I bent over her to get them in shadow and they opened. Let me in. We drifted in among the flags and stuck. The way they went down sighing before the stem! I lay down across her with my face in her breasts and my hand on her. We lay there without moving, but under us all moved, and moved us, gently up and down and from side to side."

William, too, was being embraced, enfolded by other arms. Her heart contracted.

"Tess!"

"What?"

"Where are your thoughts?" asked Laura.

"Never mind her thoughts," said William, "Listen to this Tess, your Italian sculptor was arrested on the Kurfürstendamm yesterday, ballocky naked and raving against culture. You remember, the chap you gave your watch to at the Akademie party, he must be engraved on your mind."

"I wonder, was he wearing it?" she said vaguely.

"Yes of course, that and nothing else."

"He really fancied you," clucked Laura, patting her on the shoulder.

"Just her type."

"Yes, I suppose so, and I wouldn't really be surprised at anything he does," she said recovering, laughing, "He was nervous about his exhibition that night and when he took a fancy to my watch, why, I could only fasten it onto his wrist. It was cheap, after all, a bauble bought in a fashion house. As you say, Laura, it worked like a charm."

But with the word 'charm' she had knocked over her wineglass. A pool of purple lay on the red table, reflecting the window and the trees outside. Bauble, she thought, gift. In the garden of 52 Beskinstrasse, the fish pendant lay under the leaves.

Nervously she glanced at William whose eyes were on the overturned glass. Impassively he stroked his beard.

"There is no shortage of wine." Laura remarked quickly, pouring Tess another. She wiped the table and took out a sheaf of papers from the dresser. She had been commissioned, she said, to write an article on the *Gastarbeiter* and was gathering the facts together. Greeks, Turks and Spaniards were recruited to work in West German factories. "They are despised. In the underground people turn away; they prefer the dogs on their laps." Bound by a sense of family they sent the bulk of their earnings home and lived poorly themselves. Her voice faded in the roar of a plane which appeared to nuzzle the window at first, like a lungfish in the aquarium, before passing overhead to Tempelhof Airport. This happened at regular intervals of five minutes or so, a constant reminder of isolation.

"They are badly housed," Laura went on, "I have seen their bachelor quarters. There they live for nine months of the year in cubicled misery. They can't read the safety warnings in the factories and accidents happen. My own countrymen, imagine how I feel? I know all this to be true and I will do something about it."

"You will. And you will do it beautifully," said William. With the help of a little wine he was warming up. "This chair is killing me."

"Please take another."

"I'd like to tell you about a dream I had," said Tess.

"Tell me, my dear." Laura lent forward. "I am all ears. I like that expression, all ears."

"I walk over sand dunes towards the sea. I cannot see the shore, but as I get nearer I hear the sound of something large splashing and trembling amongst stones.

At last I see the beach. Before me in the shallows lies an enormous whale, rolling over in the small waves, exposing first a white belly and then a grey back. I ask myself, is it dying? Is it dead? Then, before my astonished eyes, it turns into a gigantic ape which rises out of the sea and lopes off head down, hair matted and shoulders bowed. The whale had great beauty, the ape was grotesque."

"The whale is the soul," said Laura, "and the ape the body, the old conflict."

She is being given symbols to convey fears she dare not speak, Laura thought. Does William hear her?

"It's a parable of evolution," remarked William. "The ape interests me, he is the turning point, there's something apologetic about him, a face of great sadness, he knows he is on the perimeter of something that he cannot break through. With knowledge the clouds will clear from his face. I understand him, things have not changed that much, we are still in the jungle, swinging through the lower branches we make our choice. I drink to that. And may the giving hand never falter." With that he disappeared into his glass.

He hears all right, thought Laura, and turns his back.

She asked Tess to help her serve the meal and together they went into the kitchen.

"Funny, your dream reminds me of a Spanish copla," Laura said, leaning back on the sink, translated it goes like this:

" On the shore of the sea
A whale lay sighing,
And sighing it said
'Those who love suffer pain.' "

Tess nodded her head. How much did Laura know?

There was asparagus with homemade mayonnaise flavoured with garlic and grated lemon peel, roast duck cooked to a fine crispness, quince sauce, new potatoes and a mixed salad. She garnished the roast duck with olives, slices of orange and watercress. William was already at the table smoothing a napkin on his knee.

"Wow! High living!" he exclaimed, looking at the spread.

"Now, to get back to the jungle again," said Laura. "When you speak about choice, for a woman it's not so easy. Not for me, nor for Tess, particularly here. Take the German sexual advance. In Spain the game is played differently and I know how to handle it, but what am I to do here confronted by a blunt invitation to go to bed, that pale eye getting paler? I don't know what they are saying exactly." She said. "But I do know this much: they have no style."

"Military manoeuvres on the counterpane from an early age," William remarked. "An old nation of warriors, you zip up your fly and move on." He described a visit to a Berlin tailor. "I had ordered this pair of trousers. The tailor put a question to me which I asked my friend to translate. The question was: 'On which side do you wear your shame?' ''

Tess, commenting on the Spanish approach, said she had been amused by a compliment received on a Malaga street.

"As the man passed me he remarked 'you're so beautiful your mother must have been made of sugar and cinnamon.' Imagine that?"

"I can, my dear," said Laura, smiling and disappearing into the kitchen.

"Did you notice something?" asked William quietly, cocking an eyebrow.

"What?"

"She devoured you with her eyes."

"Oh!"

Laura's small hands weaved in and out, now and then there was a flash of amethyst; her chubby legs were crossed, her skirt rode up her thighs. She liked to talk about sex. "But I'll be glad when it's all over," she said with a sigh. She told them about her childhood, the family house outside Seville, walking through the olive groves at night. "Those trees understood the language of silence. I walked alone and fearful, my hair standing on end." In the tilled earth they found Moorish coins.

Tess looked across at William. He had never looked so handsome, she thought, confident: exuding health and energy like a man on a parapet, with the light shining upon him.

She asked if she might use the telephone to check if the children were all right. It was in the bedroom. She closed the door behind her, found it under some scented petticoats on the bed and dialled, her hand shaking. She was now distressed by her rash disposal of the pendant but knew she would never retrieve it.

Laura's clothes were half unpacked and lying on chairs, evidence of her migrant temperament.

Tess, who was having difficulty getting through to Rosalinde, thought if William was having an affair Laura surely knew about it, the Akademie people were famous gossips. She was reminded of Charles Darwin's account of the South American jungle where the noise of the insects could be heard a mile offshore, while in the forest itself there was absolute silence. She heard Laura laugh and smiled. The laugh was infectious: chortling up through countless channels it exploded her anatomy, and the black lavender bushes on the high plains of the Estremadura bent as one to the sound.

Back in the dining-room McDaid rose feeling for his cigarettes, patted his Hemingway-waistcoat — black velvet lined with pale blue silk — and strained at his pockets. "Begorrah, where are my Gauloises?" he cried. There was a tearing sound as the pocket gave. With great fuss and acute exasperation now, he plunged his hand into the inside silk pocket and, finding nothing there, ripped that downwards too. Encouraged in this performance by Laura who was whooping with laughter, he tore it off, grappled with it in the air and tossed it onto a chair with derision, while the blue silk tongues hung down.

It was then Tess returned to the room.

"Here was a thing and a very pretty thing, what have I done with this pretty thing?" he asked her smiling.

"Your husband," Laura said, "is a clown, he destroys me."

"He's adept at that," said Tess picking up the torn waistcoat and shaking with fury. "See this, Laura? A talisman." At the back of the neck was a small square of embroidery. "I made it, I made it all!"

Laura dabbed her wet cheeks and shook her head.

"William, you're shameless!"

He turned on Tess, mercurial and sober now, firing out the words: "*You have taken my fish pendant. Bad luck to you!*"

Confession

The next day William was in an explanatory mood.

"I met her at a party and we talked all night," he said, "I knew at once this was it, what I'd been looking for. She's a younger version of yourself — you should be flattered — tall and rangy, but a hard woman. I like that. Yes, and it's a good feeling to be appreciated, to receive only praise. I can do no wrong. Imagine?"

Tess could well imagine. She longed for something like that herself.

He lay down on the chaise-longue in the conservatory placing his hands languidly behind his head as if on protected ground.

"I'm resolved to make this an open affair."

"Open, what d'you mean, open?"

"Not furtive, as in the past, no hole-in-the-corner stuff."

"And me? The children?"

Jonathan was making faces at them through the window, his features smudged against the glass. Sam, playing in the hall, listened avidly.

"I know it's hard for you, but you'll find someone too, I hope. I need women to give me energy for my work, you must understand. I've simply gone ahead, you'll follow. What about that Italian sculptor, what's his name, Eduardo?"

Looking at him she thought: it suits you well to be in love, it's in your walk, you've no weight, you've never been so vital. Can I begrudge you this? If I want you to thrive, can I impose conditions? *Yes*, your blatant lack of feeling angers me, I'm jealous of your good times. Every step you take I will be there. In intimate cafes my shadow will lie under your joined hands, I'll be in the double shape on the wall as you kiss, never so constant in love, never so constant. . .

"But I love you," she said in spite of herself.

"Then return the pendant to prove it," said he slyly.

"No, never."

"Do you know what you've done? It's a present."

"So I've guessed."

"Where is it? Give me an idea. In the garden?"

"I'm not saying. I never want to see it again in my life."

"I can tell from your face it's in the garden," he

45

announced leaping up, "Your luck depends on my finding it," and went out to examine the lawn.

She took out her needlework basket and started to darn but her hands were shaking. The grass had not been cut, the pendant was minute, she was positive he'd never find it. It would be somewhere near the boundary fence, further than he would look.

After a while, thoroughly exasperated, William threw himself down on the grass and held his head shouting: "You *bitch*!"

This brought Jonathan round the house.

"What's the matter, Dad?" he asked, leaping on top of him.

"Goddamit child!" he roared, pushing him to one side, getting up and dusting his trousers.

"*Tell me!*" he shouted at Tess through the window, "*Woman!*" And, getting no answer, swept out of the front gate and away.

Jonathan, who had burst into tears, ran into the house and put his head on his mother's lap.

"He has gone again!" he wailed.

During that night a mild wind blew from the south, carrying with it the sound of Alsatian guard dogs barking on the frontier and the distant rattle of machine-gun fire from the Teltower Canal. An occasional lonely plane soared high overhead.

Then the dawn chorus reached the forest of Nicolassee

where at first light the voice of the blackbird dropped to the lake, followed by a volley of calls from the pine trees. Unheard by Tess who lay dozing, a volume of Faulkner open beside her and the companion bed empty.

She was back home again, standing on the hill at the Peddie Golf Links. As she looked into the distance the horizon seemed to leap. Small waves, pale green with manes of white like the heads of a thousand horses, rose and fell over the hills towards her. The closer the sea approached, the more menacing it became with increasing noise, until a large grey wave was poised to mount the hill where she stood, and the sky had darkened. She entered a cabin set amongst trees. Someone's refuge, newly painted, with low wooden beams and a light over the bed. A bunch of onions hung peacefully by the door. Then, as always with her dreams, there came a sequel. She found herself in the streets of a metropolis with the sea flowing down marble steps and watched, with curious detachment, two people struggle in the water and sink.

In the meantime a yellow Volkswagen had stopped at the end of Beskinstrasse. The woman driver cupped her hands around the face of the man at her side. Still tangled in the web of love's long night they embraced once again. They were taking giant strides together beyond the quotidian.

"You are so fine," she murmured. Reluctantly he got

out of the car holding her hand through the window for a moment.

"I see joy in your face," said William, "My joy. You are the best of me. Goodbye, my love. Tonight again?" She nodded, smiling. The car started once he had turned the corner and was out of sight. Putt-putt. Silence.

At 32 Beskinstrasse gilt bars of sunlight fell across the desk in the study where dust lay on the papers that had not been touched for days. Granules of light danced there in the sun's rays. Downstairs the two grandfather clocks discussed the half hour.

In the dank and early scents which rose from the garden, a wild cyclamen bloomed timidly at the foot of a pine tree. William selected a pine cone and threw it against the glass of the upstairs bedroom window. After a while his wife appeared in her dressing gown, saw him, shook her head and retreated.

"*Let me in!*" he shouted, as she pulled the sheets over her head. Oh, that I could reverse time, wake in my father's house to the unpunished day, she thought, hear the blinds going down and my mother singing to the radio.

There had never been so much effort in the wooing as the unwooing.

William raged, hunching his shoulders with his hands in his pockets. There was nowhere else to go. Excessively irritated he kicked the plants with his foot. She had become jealous and predictable.

Making an inspection of the house he found that the window to the basement washroom was loose and carefully eased himself through it.

Presently she heard his foot on the stair and went onto the landing hurling abuse.

"If only you would go away!"

"You dare lock me out of my own home!" he roared back, his eyes blazing.

"You don't belong here any more," she said, "I'm not waiting for you to make up your mind!"

"You bitch, you lock me out!" he hissed, making a grab for her as she rushed into the childrens' bedroom and got into bed with Nicolas, her teeth chattering. William crashed around looking for weapons but now that the boys had begun to wake, thought better of it and loped out.

It seemed to Tess she was fighting with her fists wrapped in thorns. One day, she thought, he will kill me. It would solve his problems if I were dead.

One day, he thought getting into his bed, one day I will go too far. She is getting in the way.

Within moments he was asleep and snoring loudly.

Hilton Hotels

"We stay in Hilton Hotels," Elke Schmidt said, applying liquid makeup to Tessa's face, "sometimes only for a weekend, for a fortnight at the most."

Tess, sitting on the edge of the bath with her eyes closed, enjoyed the touch of Elke's hands. She had come for advice on her appearance and was getting more than that.

Elke, whom Tess had met through a D.A.A.D. connection, was having an affair with a rich American businessman.

"He spares me all the time he can. Beirut, London, Paris, Rome, Frankfurt, Madrid. I go when I'm called." With soft manicured hands she smoothed in a pale mauve eyeshadow. "Of course I wear the most outrageous clothes." She laughed. "People stare."

They would stare at you anyway, thought Tess, your relaxed beauty, with your pile of blonde hair and flawless apricot skin. Using kohl, Elke emphasized the lower lids, her features fixed in concentration, breath sweet as a meadow.

"You have to watch where the line goes, when you bring it out beyond the eye always go up a little to give the suggestion of a smile. Mascara brush for the lashes, golden lipstick and a touch of rouge." Tess noted the transparency of her skin, the capillaries in the orbs of her eyes.

"You pose as man and wife?" she asked.

"No questions asked."

"Who pays?" asked Tess with one eye closed.

"Could I afford it?"

"What do you do in these Hiltons?" Was anywhere less conducive to romance?

"We stroke each other's foreheads."

"Stroke? Foreheads? Go on."

"Yes it's true, one of us is always sick."

"Sick?"

"Sick from separation."

Elke put the finishing touches to Tessa's hair.

"Now look in the mirror. I think you will be delighted with yourself."

Tess stood up and smiled at her reflection in the glass. The experiment was a success, her skin glowed, her eyes were enormous. She gave Elke a wink.

"Thanks."

"You're a little miracle," said Elke, "you look so young."

A photograph of an elderly man adorned the mantelpiece of the sitting room whom Elke identified as Bill, the American.

In the Hilton Hotels, thought Tess, they stare at Venus and the man with the crumpled face holding hands at the cocktail bar.

"Is he much older than you?" she asked.

Elke dismissed the question. "He's a good lover," she said.

"How nice."

"His hands, you know, as if through all women he has come to me." She blushed.

"And what do you do between the Hilton Hotels?"

"I live here respectably teaching English, sometimes translating."

"Would you marry, do you think?"

"No, that's impossible, his wife's in a mental asylum. Have a drink." Tess accepted a martini in a long glass.

One of those solitary women, she thought, trailing up and down institutional stairs unable to face the world, I know a little about that.

"Do you know about William's affair?" she asked Elke.

"How could I not? He makes no secret of it. What will you do? Have one too?"

"I'm not receptive. Too worried and trapped. I should leave but I've no money and then there are the children.

And where would I go, tell me? What country? I can't go back to South Africa, I'm a European now."

"You have problems. Tell me Tess, have you had affairs?"

"Yes, until I married. Then I took marriage seriously, it imposed some kind of order where there was none. Or so I thought at the time."

"We don't take it seriously here. I want a child, I'm thirty-three, getting old, could I have a child and be alone, do you think?" Her groomed appearance, her creaseless yellow suit and her decorum defied the possibility.

"Would it suit you? And what about the Hilton Hotels?"

"That's a false life. I'd gladly exchange the glamour for a child of my own."

That night, as Tess bathed her sons, she decided that, in spite of everything, she could not envy Elke. This gave her some comfort. She had relished the soft touch of her hands and thought she must be good in bed, but did she love the crumpled man? Did she in fact make a living by teaching English, or was she simply his flying courtesan? To have a child and combine both worlds might be the answer. But the world of the courtesan demanded presentation and no encumbrance, and then those calls to appetite from Istanbul and Cairo, pleasure cage to pleasure cage! No, she thought, looking down at her three sons who sat together in the bath like peas in a pod, there can be no compromise, and we are both victims. Damn these men!

Finally she lay down with the boys curled around her and read the story of Cornelius and Babar, a story of such simplicity it rocked them off before she reached the end.

In the corner of the room the hamster moved across the floor of his cage and entered the wheel to begin his tireless journey through the night.

It was to be Nicolas' ninth birthday the following day. She thought of his birth, of the blue nuns in the nursing home and the woman doctor who had arrived from the golf links dressed in slacks to deliver him into the world. He was an ingenious child: in Spain he had killed a snake by trapping its raised head in a door jamb. As Robinson Crusoe he had seen her in that white gown. "I love you too, remember that always, whatever happens," she whispered putting her lips to his cheek and easing herself out of the bed.

But once on the landing the silence of the house deafened her. She heard William's voice echo down the stairs into the hollow rooms "She gives me praise. I can do no wrong. No wrong."

Where was he now, the man who could do no wrong? Where were they now, the lovebirds? As if late for an appointment her mind flew after them pursuing them round her own vague and incorrect map of Berlin: Alexanderplatz, Krummelanke, the Kurfürstendamm. In Steglitz she found him buying a posy from a flowerseller. "For your sweetheart," the flowerwoman said as she pinned it on to the lapel of the girl with no face. No one knew his relentless pursuit better than herself. She saw them enter the Gattopardo restaurant, welcomed by the smiling waiters, guided to the same reserved table for two. Did the waiter not remember her, Tess, the shadow woman?

The hamster, too, was travelling and getting nowhere. The rasp of his wheel could be heard in the upstairs room.

Were they already in bed? Yes, she could feel the heat of them.

What she had taught William was being employed on another. She too had a part. Imagining what they did together confused and excited her. In the envelopment of flesh, she was there also.

The following day preparations for the birthday were in full swing. Even William, who had returned at dawn and spent the morning sleeping, rose to play his part.

Sam stood on the bedroom balcony and gazed down on the lawn, his short features blurred with envy.

Other people's birthdays took such a long time, he wished it was his, thought of it all year but it passed so quickly always. When was next July? He watched William pin the eagle kite to the tree. It was to be a Red Indian party, they would wear swans' feathers from the Wannsee. The white table cloth was on now, there was orange jelly in the peel, his favourite. There were cakes and watermelon, all for Nicolas. Whom did he hate more, himself or his brother? he wondered, as Tess put flowers round the birthday place, decorated the birthday chair with leaves and flowers. She'd done the same for him, too long ago.

"Sam, what's the matter?" Tess called from the lawn, "Come down and try on your headdress. Look! I think it's the best."

Sam straightened himself up, put his hands in his pockets. Suppose I'll go, he decided, biggest swans in the world.

When the party was over Sam, who had misbehaved and been chastized by his father, lay dejected and face down in the long grass under the lilac bush at the bottom of the garden with his headdress askew. The last goodbyes came drifting through to him from the front of the house. Soon he heard them cleaning up, returning the table and chairs to the kitchen.

"Presents! Presents!" shouted Nicolas in the distance, "All for me!" A spasm of misery shook him, then he felt something cold against his cheek and lifted his head. There, underneath him in the grass was the pendant William had lost. His first thought was to return it, but it glinted like magic as he turned it in the palm of his hand. He decided to keep it as a present for himself, to hide it and never tell a soul.

Aladdin had his lamp, and he had his pendant. To try its magic properties he gave it a simple task for a start.

Rubbing the smooth surface he looked up into the lilac bush. "I wish a leaf to fall!" he whispered, his heart racing. This was the test. Nothing happened then, incredibly, a small dry leaf dislodged itself from a branch and floated down. Excitedly he rubbed the gold again. "I wish Tess to look for me!"

"Sam!" she called "Sam! It's bathtime!"

"Abracadabra!" he murmured, slipping it into his pocket.

Encounter

Presenting Tessa with a handbag for her birthday, William smiled and said: "This is your Hiroshima Mon Amour". He was using the title of the erotic film to encourage her promiscuity. It would be convenient. "You must get out, meet people."

"How?" she asked, fingering the beautiful yellow leather.

"Go to a concert, buy a box of chocolates, offer them to a man sitting beside you. That's how to begin."

The children gathered round her in great excitement, they had gifts too, drawings. She looked up at him.

"I'm out of practice," she said.

One night in November she stood at the window of 32 Beskinstrasse and watched the snow. In the air and where it lay, all seemed changed to umbrellas of white and silence. The day had died, another terrible night had begun. Peace falling, but there was no peace: anguish was tearing hope into shreds. Behind her the two grandfather clocks grappled with the hour. Time present, they rang out, time past, no answers.

Suddenly she could bear it no longer. If William went out she was no longer culpable; she would too.

She put on her green coat and white boots and slipped out of the front door. The children were fast asleep. She looked at the silver birch by the garden gate.

I entrust them to your care.

The garage was empty except for her bicycle which stood in a corner, high and narrow, with yellow lines decorating the back wheels. Ten degrees below zero, bad weather for the cyclist, the street like a ploughed field with frozen furrows. The hood of her coat was up and fastened under her chin. Her nose was cold. With gloved hands she grasped the handlebars firmly and chose the footpath, cleared with ashes and salt. The going was not easy.

Fine snow clung to the metal fences, to the garden gates, to the locks where the keys had been turned. The last footsteps on the paths were erased, long icicles hung from the porticoes where front doors were locked and barred. White-crested evergreens stood in the odourless gardens, and a russet apple still hung on a high branch at the corner of the road.

She dismounted at the downward steps.

"Ah, you live near the Rehwiese," people said with envy, "The meadows."

It was a short ride across the dimly lit path. The Rehwiese stretched out on each side, white meadows now, sloping down to a frozen stream where the hawthorn grew. The poplars, beech and silver birch, heavy with snow, rose out of the cold mist.

She came to the rise and the great houses of Nicolassee and, at last to the festive lights of the S-Bahn, the overhead railway, left her bicycle near the ticket office and went up to the platform.

"You are going out alone again?" the ticket collector asked, blowing his hands to get them warm.

"My husband is waiting for me in town," she lied.

He smiled as she walked away.

The train rattled through the Grunewald towards the Zoo Station. Against the black moving forests she studied her face in the glass, behind which the city slowly appeared with a perforation of lights.

Entering "Die Lupe", the art cinema, she bought a box of chocolates and, in the dark, found a seat. The film had already started. A student, dressed in petticoats flew along a Madrid street on a bicycle. Suddenly he hit the kerb and fell over. Deathly pale, blood coming from his mouth, he lay on the pavement. A girl at a top window gasped at the sight. In a moment she was down in the street to get a closer look. The crowd drew apart and she took him up to her apartment. Buñuel's "*Un Chien Andalou*" she had seen before.

Tessa became aware she was seated next to a large man. From the corner of her eye she saw his brooding head and bulky frame. She liked his presence, the space he occupied. As she raised the chocolates on her lap he stared at the screen.

The student lay on the bed in the girl's apartment. Suddenly he opened his dark eyes. His aspect was fearsome; chalk white skin, jutting eyebrows. He looked around wildly and pursuing the girl to the door, wrenched her hand off the doorhandle. She rolled her eyes as he pulled the shoulder of her dress down and covered her breast with his hand. There was a close-up of the hand on her breast and her round white shoulder.

Tess felt as if her breath had left her. She noticed the powerful hand on the arm of her chair, long-boned and still. Inexplicable tears came to her eyes. Leaning forward she laid her forehead upon it. Presently she felt the gentle pressure of his other hand upon her head. Feeling the moisture of her eyes, he lent forward and said quietly: "You are unhappy."

She lifted her head and saw his features for the first time. A serious man, greying at the temples. Fifty-five perhaps? No frivolity in the set of his face: hooded, kindly eyes. He looked at her with interest and more than curiosity, as if surprised. Strangely familiar, he thought, English perhaps. An attractive, private face. Although she looked girlish he suspected she might be older than she appeared.

After this brief exchange they continued to watch the film. He turned his hand upwards, the palm was soft and undulating, she accepted the invitation and placed hers in his. When the film ended he turned to her. "Do not go", he said in English. She nodded, and they left together.

"What's troubling you?" he asked. "Do please tell me!" They were seated in a coffeehouse at a table against the wall. "Well," she said slowly, looking for words, "My marriage is at an end. My husband has found someone else. I feel lost. I know no one in Berlin. I look around, other people's pleasure my loss, everywhere, you understand. I feel I am falling."

"Jealousy," he said quietly, turning the coffee cup in his hand. "A solemn education. Darkness, with bats. I've been there. A bad time for you to be looking around. Feelings run against time." He now became very animated and smiled. "I already know your face, but I need your name."

"Tessa," she said, "South African. You know my face? We've never met."

"You will understand, I hope, later . . . Tessa." He savoured her name with delight, "Perfect. Your name a perfect present. Your present to me. I don't wish to explain except that I make my own films, it has to do with that. Would you permit me to invite you home, I find it difficult to give advice, but I could show you a film of mine which might have a meaning for you."

They walked up the broad Kurfürstendamm. The expensive cafes extended onto the pavement, enclosed in glass. Through the misted windows waiters could be seen flitting about. The teenage whores stamped their well-shod feet in the snow. With their fur coats curled up to their noses they called to each other.

"You should be here in the early hours, when the actors, actresses and strip girls meet their friends in the cheap taverns. *That* is when real gaiety begins. Here", he said taking her arm, "here we turn left."

The side street was deserted. She stopped in her tracks. "Please. Don't hesitate."

After a while they mounted an outside staircase where a cat gleamed for a moment and was gone.

"My place," he said, opening the door. Her anxious presentiments faded when she saw the room, lined with books. The windows over the street were covered by curtains falling in long pure folds of white. The furniture was low and generous. An orderly man, Tess thought, at peace with himself. There was an open envelope on a table addressed to Piers Moller.

"Our encounter tonight," said Piers, getting her a glass of wine, "is beyond coincidence for both of us, I hope. You must be curious." He brought in a film projector and set up the screen. "I like Buñuel for his extravagant images. He's a tease." When he had the equipment ready he switched off the light.

"Tell me what you see, please," he said, "exactly, as if I were blind. The soundtrack has Schubert's Quintet in C Major, Opus 163 — the Adagio — an old recording. Intentionally old."

The film began with a moving mist. Indeterminate shapes passed across the screen. A pale winter sun probed through.

"I see," she said, "A lagoon. The water shines where the sun falls. To one side is a high pile of logs. There is someone there. A young woman."

He leant forward. "How do you see her?"

"She seems familiar. Square shoulders, hair in two bunches. Tall. She enjoys moving, it is part of her nature. Like me."

"Yes."

"She mounts the logs, wet and slippery, taking great care not to fall, now stands at the top, her legs apart, collar turned up against the wind. The scene opens out. What I took to be a lagoon is the estuary of a large river.

Limitless water.

Small canoes pass below, swiftly paddled and borne on by the current. The sky and water are grey, the boats are grey, the boatmen covered in long grey wet hair. Are they boatmen, or are they dogs?"

"Go on," he said, "I'm listening."

"The girl crouches down to get a clearer view. One of the boatmen turns round. Now I see him closely, his nose is like a muzzle, pointed. His features twitch from energy and strain. Although he does not speak, his face tells me they live like this, arduously, always travelling fast. He flicks the hair from his face like an Afghan hound, shivering slightly, dips the paddle down and continues on." Tess leant back in her chair. "It occurs to me he belongs to water, like a polyp to a rock.

Now the girl is alone there. She sits down on the logs, watching the boats passing below, like moving dots, and the mists swirl down once more."

The music and images faded away and they sat in the dark. Tess laughed. "She is uncommonly like me. She will watch forever. Where did you make the film? Where did you find me?"

"Norway, I made the film last winter, but it only comes alive now with you, your name and the title which will be 'Vision for Tessa'. You are receptive, I thought you would be."

"I'm looking for signs," Tess said. "I see the lagoon becomes an estuary, things will go on."

"Yes," he switched on the light.

She smiled, looking up. "And we live travelling at enormous speed. Those are your messages to me." He was pleased.

"I felt I had been there before."

"You may have been. As they say, the gaze is sometimes older than the eye."

When the ornate clock on the bookshelf chimed 11.30, she was startled and rose up from her chair.

"Don't go now," he protested. "You cannot leave so suddenly, nothing is resolved."

She took his hand. "You are wrong," she said, "please forgive me. Let us part without false hopes. I mustn't miss the last train. The children."

He raised the palms of his hands and tilted his head to one side.

"Very well," he said, "the children."

Returning on the S-Bahn once again, she warmed her feet on the radiator under the old wooden seat and, with her head thrown back, looked at her reflection in the glass, and cursed her honest face.

William stood at the window in the childrens' room, watching Tess return on her bicycle, the front wheel wobbling as she engaged the frozen, rutted path. He imagined he heard her weep and was filled with remorse. "And yet," he thought, "I will do it again. I will do it all again. My vows break before your eyes, my love."

Christmas Party

From the top of a bus Tessa had noticed a large laurel bush beside the main highway. On the apex of the bush sat a pigeon on an old nest. The nest was falling apart, the bush tumbled down its large soiled leaves to the ground and shook as the traffic passed, but still the pigeon sat. There I am on my old nest, she thought, only a matter of time before we slide to the ground and lie in a heap.

"Walter and I will look after the children, don't worry now and have a good time," said Rosalinde. Under her arm Tess carried a long red tartan skirt she had borrowed which she planned to wear with a red pullover. The invitation to the Christmas party was a half-hearted one passed on to her by William. "You can go or not, as you please," he said. A party at the Akademie, however, was not something she cared to miss. She liked the place: it was a vast complex of buildings dedicated to the arts, a happy mixture of austerity and grandeur. Two large theatres served also for lectures and films, the foyer and entrance halls were used for exhibitions, and beyond these were stairs and lifts to studio flats for artists and writers, some of grand proportions and smaller rooms for the casual visitor to Berlin. It was a lively place.

In the vast hall adjoining the theatre the Christmas party was in full swing with a string orchestra on a dais, several bars and waiters serving a variety of tempting foods. Pennants were strung from wall to wall. William was in great form, bouncing on the balls of his feet. A bad sign. Tess, with the nose of a sleuth, detected danger.

A man stepped out of the crowd. "Splendid!" he exclaimed at the sight of William. "Here we are."

William introduced Tess: "This is Rudi, and here we have. . ." "My Irish friend" someone said, "I forget your name, *bitte schön?*"

A girl in her early twenties approached Tess and announced herself as Anneliese Rombard. She was tall, expensively dressed in a silver jerkin open to the midriff which quivered as she breathed, black sheath trousers and silver shoes. Her hair was long and brown.

"I have heard much about you," she said.

Indeed, thought Tess, noting her remarkable, heavily made-up eyes which held their gaze too long. Beauties had this knack, when looking should have stopped, of consuming you in the vacancy of their dark pupils.

"You have travelled so much," sighed Anneliese.

Really? Tess thought as she tried to look past her, but each time the girl was in the way. Was she hiding someone?

Rudi took Tess by the arm. He was a serious man.

"Let us dance," he said seriously. He was a doctor, he said. It was a profession of decision-making, but he liked parties, they took his mind off his work, he liked to see the circus in full swing, it provided a balance. Tess half heard him. Over his shoulder she looked for William.

"The girl Anneliese. You are old friends?" she asked casually.

"Oh yes, very old friends, I have known her for years. I am very fond of her, but she has one fault, she loves power."

Suddenly William emerged at the far end of the hall tugging Anneliese by the hand. Cornfield frolics. Thinking himself unobserved he sat on a high stool and pulled her over to him. Tess was riveted. There was no mistaking a long intimacy.

"Your countryman, Dr Barnard," went on Rudi, "was visiting Berlin the other day. Of course his work as a heart transplant specialist is acclaimed, but he was disliked as a man."

Tess felt she was drowning. William was drowning too. The orphans stood terrified, biting their nails on the shore. She excused herself and crossed the floor.

"So it is you!" she accused Anneliese.

The couple drew apart.

"I see it in your eyes."

Affecting absence William said nothing.

"What is this you can see in the eyes?" demanded Anneliese brazenly, "You can see nothing."

"I see love, but it is not so simple," replied Tess, her face breaking up. She turned and went slowly across the floor and up the stairs to the cloakroom. Locking herself into a cubicle she sat on the seat and wept. Wept for the collapse of her world so far held together by its small bright hopes.

How long she remained there she did not know, but when she emerged William was waiting for her in the corridor.

"Party's over," he announced coldly, "time to go."

The revellers and orchestra had long since left, streamers and party hats littered the floor. They went through the swing doors and out into the cold night, down the old deserted streets towards the river Spree, Tess walking slowly, her eyes scalded, her mind jinking, like someone led to execution.

Ancient buildings heavy with cornice and architrave spoke a bleak history. There are no ordinary lives, she thought, there is no ordinary sleep, the empty rooms dream of occupation, I will knock on the door of the concierge and receive no answer, I will call my name to no effect. I have been here before. I do not recall the details. Beside me walks the hangman picking his way through the snow like a dancer, he will wait for the right moment to perform his task. Or will I do it for him?

Oppressed by these black thoughts she was hardly prepared for the bizarre incident which happened next.

When they reached the river Spree William pointed to a phone booth on the other side, and suggested they call a taxi. Tess was aware they were not alone. In the shadows two men embraced on the pavement.

"What?"

"Taxi," he said, "phone booth, over there. Will you do it?"

She crossed the bridge. With the receiver to her ear, she cleared the glass with her glove and peered out at the swirling night; the vague shape of the bridge, the reflections of the streetlamps fractured on the ice. She could see no-one. She gave up ringing and began to cross the bridge, when she heard a voice cry from the far bank: "Albert! Albert! Where are you?" and to her horror a sobbing, drowning voice replied from the river below her. "I'm here, but it's too late! too late!" At which there was a splash and crack of ice as the man on the bank hurled himself into the water also.

"Help!" he shouted. "Albert!"

Tess ran across and found William taking off his overcoat at the water's edge.

"What's going on?"

"Attempted suicide." he said, casting the coat down the slippery bank and holding onto a sleeve. "Luckily the water isn't deep enough."

"Here!" he called out "Come here, help is here!"

There was a silence which seemed endless, then slowly there came the sound of both men swimming and wading towards them. Presently two heads became visible. They pulled themselves up with difficulty, using the coat as a rope and, with no word of thanks to their rescuers, embraced and walked off, drenched and clasped together.

"Well that's that!" said William. His overcoat was soaked through and they were miles from anywhere.

By good fortune a police car appeared at this point and offered to take them home.

The policeman remarked on the way that attempted suicide and suicide itself were commonplace events.

Kiss and Farewell

Waiting for the iron to warm up, Tess read again the telegram from her brother in South Africa: DAD DIED PEACEFULLY TODAY WEDNESDAY. She thought how last thing at night he'd go round the house putting out the lights. Now they were out for him, all light, forever. She'd sensed something wrong from his last letters, the small neat handwriting going sideways across the page. Pneumonia in the end. Death? Her father? Unreal. Five words. A change? No, she did not feel a change. What she had most feared all her life had finally no impact at all compared to her sense of personal catastrophe.

As the control button was broken she turned the iron up in her hand, spat on the plate and watched the beads of saliva spin and sizzle on the surface, giving off a smell like burning hair. Guiding the point of the iron round the buttons, pulling and pressing the seams flat, she brought the old family clothes back to shape again. Once there'd been comfort in it, now it seemed yet another useless occupation. Fear, coupled with an almost hysterical sense of the dramatic, whipped her thoughts along.

Marriages were broken two-a-penny, there was no provision for her. Private bonds of tenderness, of shared experience and common suffering were puffballs, blown away by the briefest wind. With the birth of her sons she'd learnt to measure, to preserve, to build: skills which had not come easily. Shoulders broadening to the task, heart rejoicing in purpose, she walked differently. Each child was a celebration. Of what? Puffballs?

She had the flavour of doom in her mouth like rusty nails. No consequence! Stupidity! Stupidity! Applying pressure on the iron, she broke a button.

I am a kind of joke, she thought, the one who buys a ticket for a train which no longer runs.

It was with relief she heard the front door bell ring, and crossed the dimly-lit hall to answer it. What she saw took her aback. A man stood on the path under a halo of light. He had a camel hair coat, blonde hair, full beard and silver breath. Tess, who thought it was a heavenly visitation, shielded her eyes.

"Tess!" he said, "Tess! Don't you recognize me?"

"My God, Svend! Forgive me, you appeared so strange for a moment. You're the last person I expected to see here. Please come in."

"It's not so far from Denmark, you know." He laughed, taking off his gloves and stamping the snow from his boots.

"An embrace," he demanded, enveloping her.

They sat in the dining-room facing each other, hands clasped over the table, talking about the past. William had once sourly remarked he was Denmark's answer to Hemingway. The description was accurate, he had the build, the hair, the greying beard.

"What brings you here?"

"I know Berlin well from happy times in my youth. I come back to visit it now and again. This house is very quiet, where's everyone?"

"The children're visiting friends."

"And William?"

"Out."

"Good, I'm glad he's not here. I never took to him. I came to see you."

"How did you find my address?"

"Word gets around."

"And I thought I was forgotten! How long is it? Three years since Spain?"

"Something like that."

"Down you came from the mountains," she said, "to the Costa del Sol, and sat at the bar tables, dispensing bonhomie. That's how I like to remember you."

"That coast nearly killed me. Remember my bronchitis?"

"Yes. The last time I saw you, you were really ill."

"I thought I was dying. That cough, the flies of Andalucia," he said, filling his pipe and frowning. "Under merciless attack. Losing hope, more than you ever knew. Paranoia. Then you appeared at the door, a ray of hope."

"I did nothing."

"Your presence I could believe in. Funny too. You sat beside my bed and caught the flies with your hands, one after the other. I'll never forget that." He laughed. "My eyes popped out of my head."

"I'm a devil with flies. How are things now?"

"Things are going very well. I'm translating Shakespeare. As an old respected writer I get a handsome grant from the Danish Government to disappear into my work." He had a sing-song voice and a pedantic manner. One of those people ancient from the start, always ancient, she couldn't imagine him young.

"You were always disappearing, as you say, into your work," she smiled, "like a mole."

"Worth it, I've great good fortune. And what about you?" He fixed her with his china blue eyes. "You're pale, Tess, why so pale?"

"I'm in bad shape. Read this." She handed him the crumpled telegram.

"My dear, I'm so sorry." He raised his head slowly, reluctant to meet her eyes.

"I think the funeral must be today," she said in a faraway voice. "I don't know what to do with grief. I'll never find that kind of love again, yet feel nothing. I envy him the death of thought."

"How can you say that?"

"My own life's falling apart rapidly. William's having an affair."

"Not again?"

"Snipping the ties. I am reminded of a painting in the National Gallery by Emil Nolde. In the foreground is a bank of hydrangeas in full bloom. You look through the hydrangeas across the wide lawns to a path which leads up to the front door of a house. High trees stand at each side of this house. The owner welcomes his guests under the lamplight, it's early evening. Such *normality* from which I'm always excluded. How long, I wonder, have I been on the outside peering through that hedge? Years. Now I wonder what will become of us? Myself and the children. We've no home after Berlin."

"What about South Africa?"

"I can't go back."

"And this girl?"

"A Berliner. I've met her."

"Of course, William saw to that."

"It happened."

"And?"

"The comparison's woeful. I'm not immune to the beauty of my own sex, Svend. When I confronted her she denied everything, of course. At first I thought her unique, now I see her everywhere: striding in front of me down the road, the heel of a trim shoe disappearing round a corner. She sits opposite me in the train. She's everywhere at once, walking down the Kurfürstendamm in a white raincoat and shopping at Nicolassee half an hour later, dressed in green. She must be a type or I'm obsessed."

"Poor Tess, of course you're obsessed, how can you help it? Come to me in Klostergaard." He took a photograph out of his wallet of a large house overgrown with ivy.

"A fine place, don't you think? Join me there, I would look after you and the children. Don't despair. It's strange, but I find increasingly that women use me as their confidant — a role I enjoy. I see now, for instance, that I was drawn here because you needed me." There came the sound of children's voices, then a pummelling on the door.

"They're back," she said smiling.

As she opened the door all three boys talked at once.

"Come and see Svend," she said, "you remember Svend, from Spain?"

They stood at the door. They did not remember him. Svend was a childless man. Not only did he not understand children, he was afraid of them, something she had forgotten. He gave them a nervous smile which was not returned.

"I'll see to you in a minute," she called as they rushed noisily up the stairs.

"It will be their supper time soon," he said.

"Yes, do stay and eat with us."

"I think not. I must go to my hotel and change, but I'd like to come back later and take you out. I don't like the idea of you being alone, particularly tonight. How would you know Berlin is a city of delights? I know what we'll do, we'll go on the town, you and I, it will take you out of your troubles. When are the children asleep?"

A festive shaft of yellow light fell across the snow-covered pavement outside the Galerie Grishka. Svend took her hand and led her in. The office was being used as a bar, beside which an elongated negro with a peony in his buttonhole, sat on a high stool with his legs crossed. Languid, and cultured of voice, he appeared to be the exotic boyfriend of the gallery owner Madame Grishka. A mixed exhibition of paintings hung on the walls, artists she did not know.

Svend was greeted as an old and distinguished friend — "Please meet a famous Danish writer, translator of Shakespeare," Madame Grishka oozed, offering him round like a tasty dish. George Grosz knew his Berlin, thought Tess, these were his characters: lewd, affected and cruel. An old and wicked sparkle came from the veteran cast of private viewers. Did the smell of wood frames, varnish, flowers and scent excite the business deal? Their noses dilated. Tess was glad of anonymity, glad of time to think. She turned the glass in her hand — Beaujolais, woody red — and thought back to the afternoon.

"Here you see snow on the ground," she had said to the children, "but in South Africa it's summertime and very hot. The Xhosa men come riding into Peddie from the hills in a whirl of dust, gallop round the statue of Queen Victoria. Wearing broad hats and red blankets, they trot past the King's Theatre on their way to the shops. This happens every Saturday, but on this day, something else is happening, something to do with us." She wondered what the impact might be. "In Alexander Road a coffin will be brought quietly into the cool church. The coffin of my father, for he is dead." Her mouth felt dry. "The minister will say a few kind words and a prayer over him, and he will be taken by his friends, all dressed in black with top hats, to the cemetery which is among pine trees. My father, your grandfather, a lovely man."

Nicolas alone had tears in his eyes, he'd noticed the break in her voice.

Tess felt a hand on her arm. Beside her was an elderly man with a bow tie and melting eyes.

"My dear," he said, "you have hardly touched your wine, you are far away. May I introduce myself, Thomas Weber. I will stand by to fill your glass for you. You have been in Berlin long?"

"Six months."

"And you are here alone?"

"No, with my three children."

He turned to his middle-aged companion and shook his head, speaking softly to her in German.

"He is very upset you have children," the woman said, "He doesn't believe in children."

"You see," said Thomas Weber becoming expansive. "It is against all erotic principles, this business of children. All the work and time you spend on them. There is the animal in you, what do you do with that? The responsibility is too much. Do you have lovers? I sigh when I think of the possibilities of your beautiful body. Wasted. I know how to treat women, look at Maria here," he turned to his smiling companion. "Look at that moist mouth and that rosy glow coming from her cheeks. There is no question about it, she is fulfilled. Women, you know, were meant to thrill."

Tess was amused by the unexpected verb, like the twang of a guitar. Love in Berlin was highly advertized, could be bought for the price of a deodorant or the whiteness of a shirt. Love smiled, would always dance. This rosy glow was nearer to the truth.

"It's a little early for Chez Nous," said Svend, blowing on his hands as they tramped through the snow, "Never mind, it will liven up later."

As they entered the club through velvet curtains, a canned voice sang 'His eyes are blue, his hair is yellow, gee but he's a charming fellow'. Behind the bar a golden female whistled along to the song perfunctorily sponging the gilt counter with strong, well-manicured hands. Her vermilion nails flashed to and fro. She acknowledged their arrival by raising her enormous false eyelashes for a moment. Another peroxide blonde with loose curls worked the cash register with a heavy hand, shaking the bronze cherubs in ornate relief. The walls were upholstered in pink leather, and the pink mirrors and heavily draped lights spoke of legendary dissipation. To the right of the bar, and set back, was an intimate theatre with an elevated stage in semi-darkness. Was the central heating exhaling Chanel No 5, wondered Tess.

Sitting on a high stool in the far corner, a brunette with a top-heavy bouffant hairstyle and legs crossed, pouted into a compact mirror in such a way that those present could admire her sensuous lips. Tessa looked questioningly at Svend. The place was very bizarre.

"Women don't come here to preen," he said, "only transvestites". Tess was, in fact, the only valid female present. The bar "girls" conversed in cracked voices like a pair of prime bitches.

"They are saying," he translated, "that the pouting girl has had an operation to make her a complete female. That one envies her, the other crudely says 'it's kiss and farewell — who wants that?' " He laughed.

Memories of her father returned to Tess: the deliberation of his hands — large, bony, sensual hands, immaculately manicured by the lady at Dobson's Hair Salon. Once he had peeled grapes for her, one of her first memories, peeled each grape, taken out the pips and popped it into her mouth "For you, Billy", her pet name. She imagined his funeral. In the crisp dry heat the procession crackled its way over the bubbling tarmac, proceeded along Alexandra Road by the disused railway track and the old mill, turned left at the end of town down the avenue of dusty pines, past the old hockey field and through the iron gates. Her father's friends stood bowed around the grave, their hats tucked under their arms, and she who loved him best was absent.

"How do you fancy them, our two hostesses?" Svend asked. They were drinking crême de Menthe with ice, in long green glasses.

"Those two broads? Why, they disappoint me," Tess replied. "If I were them I would choose an exotic image, it's easy to find such women, with hatchet features and voices to match. After all, great expense has been put into their appearance only to give a rather commonplace effect. They could be tea ladies in a London hospital wheeling a trolley down the corridor and bickering about their jobs, they have that much distinction, except," she was forced to add "for the overt sexplay." For, at this point the curtains admitted a newcomer: an elegant man in a black cape with a small goatee beard and devouring eyes. The two "ugly sisters" fell into a flurry of positioning and flounce, batting their eyelids and the cherubs on the cash register trembled. Here was an habitué, certainly, and a favoured one at that.

"Perhaps it is not a matter of choosing an image so much as being limited to the female they already have inside them," Svend said. "What I find charming is the total lack of compromise, the liberation. These transvestite clubs, you know, are an old Berlin institution, in fact they cater for a very pedestrian public on the whole. Married couples, such as you see over there, come for an evening's diversion and I expect they are never disappointed."

True enough, by this time the company had expanded. There was a middle-aged couple beside them engaged in conversation with a young woman who could have been their daughter, a ravishing girl with an innocence in her wide eyes which set her apart from the rest.

Sentimentality was dangerous, Tess thought to herself, she had inherited it from her father and was passing it on to her children. She remembered the sweet occasions she had shared with him: the birthday chair a throne of flowers and leaves, the midnight services at Easter they attended together in different churches — the mysteries. At Christmas time they'd gathered wild berries, leaves to decorate the rooms.

"Do not restrain your tears, Billy, unshed tears fall back into the heart, you know, and leave deep wounds." He had said and she had many times seen him weep openly in sorrow and happiness — almost Russian.

It was not altogether bad, this sense of ritual and respect for feeling, but it would not serve her now. Bone and muscle were required.

Several couples now rose, drink in hand, and made their way towards the tables encircling the small, now spotlit stage. Music came from behind a screen, introductory notes which promised something frivolous. The bar girl who had deplored kiss and farewell appeared from behind the screen in a state of semi-undress. Her pink sequinned "gown" covered little and revealed too much. Black hair sprouted on her inner thighs and she had rather heavy shoulders, but it was evident she had breasts. Truant soft rolls at the neck put her at roughly forty. She sang a German song, the words of which escaped Tess, but the meaning was clear. Using the microphone as a penis she not only sang to it, she cajoled, stroked and kissed it; Tess feared she might swallow it altogether. She whipped the flex around her like a snake. It slapped the floor and shook in all its length. The gravel voice implied desperate measures if she couldn't keep her man. She was a natural comic and received great applause.

They were still sitting on bar stools where the counter curved towards the stage when someone touched Tessa's back. She was sitting behind Svend holding her glass on the counter with her left hand when she felt her arm gently stroked from behind and a breath on her hair. The man with the goatee beard was behind her. "Cherie," he murmured looking ahead, slipping his hand round her waist. Svend turned round at that moment and the man moved away.

"You weren't expecting that, were you?" he whispered.

The music thrummed out the opening bars to 'The Man I Love'. Languidly, and with perfect grace, the young girl, who had come with the middle-aged couple, took the microphone and began to croon with her eyes closed.

The more outrageous the performance the better Svend liked it, but Tess felt more alone and alienated than ever before.

Night flowers

When Svend rang to say goodbye, he was cheerful. "Berlin always rejuvenates me," he said, "and thank you for your company, it meant so much. I've always found you edifying, Tess. Remember the invitation to Klostergaard still stands, you can come to me. Take heart and keep that in mind."

Tess knew she would never go and, as she put the receiver down, something snapped inside her. Looking gravely into the mirror she fingered her lank hair and said to herself "edifying", remember that.

On her way to the shops that day she passed a phone booth where a woman wept, shouting into the receiver, holding it tightly with red hands as if it were a lifeline that had failed and in the supermarket, reaching up for a bunch of grapes, she happened to glance into the angled mirror above her and noticed, at the back of the shop, an immaculate young woman sobbing silently into the freezer.

This parade of cracked hearts was soon joined by a shabby, middle-aged woman with a fallen hemline talking loudly to herself on the S-Bahn station platform, shaking her heavy bags, first one then the other, and stamping her foot, "*Nein!*"

Tess, sitting on a bench waiting for the train was mesmerized. She too talked to herself by now, rehearsing what she would say to William, but when she got home the words died in her mouth. Had they died for this woman on the platform, too? William blatantly spent the nights with Anneliese now and came home to sleep by day. The children, busy with their friends, seemed unperturbed. One day in the kitchen she reproached him.

"We cannot afford your good time, where's the money for the housekeeping? Where's it gone?"

He turned on her, his features twisted with rage. "You longsuffering, ungenerous bitch!" he roared, knocking her down and pummeling her head on the floor. "Let me disfigure your face!"

The attack was brutal. As she lay, covering her head with her arms, she wondered what value her face had and why she bothered. Her endurance was slipping, she'd lost all self-esteem. She was hurtling downwards with no inclination to save herself.

It became more and more difficult for her to return home and one evening, knowing that William would be in, she decided to stay away. On the bus route she had noticed a Bavarian inn, heavily gabled with green shutters, with "Guest House" written in large letters over the entrance. To one side was a pavement bar where the flap was raised and drinks served to the standing clientele, mainly men. There she stopped.

The place seemed shabbier at close quarters. A waiter cleaned glasses with a soiled cloth.

"Can I have a room for the night?" she asked timidly.

He looked her over, this woman in a shapeless woollen suit, white boots and an open Loden coat, in one hand a furled umbrella, in the other a patent leather bag, cheeks stained, with nowhere to go written all over her face. We'll take the stains from your cheeks, he thought, smiling to himself as he gave the counter a cursory wipe.

"Could you wait please? The Manager will be around soon."

Presently a young balding man appeared who introduced himself as the proprietor. He put out a hand which on contact gave her the shudders. He did not take his hand away, it slid out of hers like some boneless wet animal. Of course they had a room for her, he said smiling obsequiously. When did she want it?

"Now," she said, her mouth in a little firm line turning down at the edges, "if you please." He explained it wasn't yet ready, but would she come upstairs to register her passport? The stairs were at the back of the building and as he led her up to his room she had that ghastly feeling on her skin again. The place was cluttered with possessions, the sideboard stacked with china and dirty glassware, a wardrobe spewing out soiled clothes — sordid relics from parents — worn couch. Against the window a filthy and unmade bed. What kind of a place was this?

Now he was anxious to get rid of her. Disturbed by her eyes, he went out to chivvy the maid.

She finally locked herself into a most impersonal room, through which many people had passed leaving an unpleasant smell like old exhausted breath. There were two bleak beds with a light between. Outside the window a sapling which caught the streetlight seemed to bear flowers: large, white night flowers.

She lay down on the bed next to the window looking at the tree. She would leave William, she told herself, split the family and take a child away with her. Which child? Jonathan needed her most. In her mind she put him in the other bed. There they lay, the two of them, like two little ships setting out into the night. But no, Jonathan wept for his brothers. Take two then, she thought, which? Nicolas or Sam? Sam was the more vulnerable, she would take him. She put him with Jonathan. They were happy there together, and the tree blazed in lifting its cup flowers, but in the distance the abandoned Nicolas howled for his brothers. No, it would be impossible, she would have to leave them together, separation would haunt them always. She would have to go alone, she decided, as a tear burned down her cheek, followed by an explosion of dry sobs from her chest. She fell asleep while the tree kept watch outside the window.

At midnight she was woken by sounds on the landing.

Someone bumped against her door, then there were two, now three men laughing quietly, their glasses clinking on the floor. There was a gentle tap on her door.

"Fräulein, let us in."

Would the door hold? She pulled up her knees to her chest in alarm, looking at the chink of light.

She clearly heard their laughter and voices whispering, asking themselves whether she slept, whether she was English. One declared he had always wanted an English girl, another agreed. She had arrived alone, he said, with an umbrella, at which there was much laughter. Then they began to sing softly at first, what sounded like a German drinking song. She relaxed, convinced there was no real threat, that the door would hold. The song got louder, erratic, out of tune, a kind of howling. "They are howling at the moon," she thought to herself, "an English moon crystal clear and faraway, I am their moon." She smiled to herself. Light, very light she felt, dry as a biscuit, as she dozed off again.

At dawn she sprang up wondering where she was. There outside the window was the sapling. Not a single flower, merely a few last leaves of autumn, waiting to fall.

Friends had passed through from Sweden on their way to Spain, admirers of William's work. They went for a walk on the frozen lake of Nicolassee, the friends taking snaps of William as if she did not exist. Realizing she was superfluous she trailed behind, covering the whorls the skaters had left with her ponderous boots. Then they came upon a square which had been cut in the ice to reveal its depth. Layers of ice denser and whiter at the surface, going blue-green down to the black water below, each stratum with its leaves and particles.

Memory's like that she thought, locked and frozen, time's colouring preserved.

Proceeding to a log cabin where a fire blazed in the grate they ordered mulled wine. Through the window Tess could see the expanse of ice, the dark slopes around the lake, and in the distance the square in the ice, its cruelly defined edge, like the photograph which would not contain her.

By this time she felt no constraint in company, tears fell down her cheeks into her glass while William and his friends laughed and talked together as if she were absent.

She tried to seek out Laura Aventura and took the U-Bahn to Tegel but couldn't find the street. There were no pedestrians of whom she could ask the way. Finally she rang at the gate of a strange house which had a formal garden and a long path to the front door. A disembodied voice spoke from the gatepost enquiring who she was, then she saw a maid descend the stairs dressed in apron and cap who took out a large ring of keys from her pocket and began unlocking doors. A hostile face appeared at an upstairs window. By the time the maid had opened the front door Tess had already fled.

Above the U/Bahn station was a small copse of pines intersected by paths. Snow lay on the ground, etched the trees. Now and then a wad of snow fell from its branch with a puff. Along these paths she trod, head bowed down. She was reluctant to leave the wood, coming to a clearing she would take another path to wind her back again. When someone crossed her path she turned her stained face away. Below her she could hear the rumbling of trains, there was also a roaring darkness in her head. I am both the corpse in the funeral cart and the single mourner following behind, shaking with conspicuous grief, she thought. If I was asked why I wept there could be no single answer. But no one did.

With the sound of another train below it became very plain what she should do. Taking out an icy, drenched handkerchief from her pocket she wiped her eyes and streaming nose, went down to the station and got her ticket. Cheap enough, 50 pfennigs. There were few people on the platform. She placed herself in the centre and walked to the edge. The rails began to sing. It will come in fast enough, she thought, I'll step forward, close my eyes and fall. The sound of the oncoming train increased, she closed her eyes, moved forward. The noise burst in her head with a million sparks, a final shattering.

Dead at last. Pain gone. Silence.

But no. There she was, standing at the edge, the train gone and the platform empty. She had not moved.

Decision

It was as if the precious details which made up her life had been erased and she was starting from nothing. But by finding nothing, Tess found the strength to leave.

As she turned into Beskinstrasse, she could hear the children playing at the Hindemanns. With a sense of relief she found the house empty, that life was proceeding without her.

She cleared away the toys in the hall, went upstairs to make the beds and cleaned the house impersonally, like a maid, with a finality of movement, mechanical and precise. She briefly wondered whether the children had missed her, but she felt no emotion or guilt. The difficult decision to go without them had already been taken. She comforted herself with the thought that she was leaving them together in a good warm house, the best they'd ever had, and the clocks, which had marked her solitude, would chime without her.

When she'd finished the cleaning she went down to the kitchen and made herself coffee, lit a cigarette and stared out of the window at the sodden garden.

There was little in her mind but what she had to do. She planned like a thief would plan a robbery, with the same attention to detail, sense of timing, composure and stealth. In fact, she was to organize her departure better than anything she had organized in her life before. Money had arrived from her father's estate and her neighbours would be her accomplices.

What was the point of marriage anyhow? They were seated back to back in Phoenix Park, Dublin with the deer grazing around them, when William proposed. His solemnity and silence attracted her from the start. He courted her with cheese omelettes in a bedsitter the size of a cupboard. She was the strong one then, worldly and experienced, capable of earning a living. William liked this in her. Although he deplored the idea of children he'd been a solicitous father at first. When they were able to interpret each other's dreams the perfect balance seemed to have been achieved: people said they looked alike. At a party someone said of them, "I wonder which is the cruel one?" a remark which had puzzled her. When he began to earn a living and received recognition for his work, things changed. Of this Tess was only too aware, but she was the guardian of the peace he needed and burrowed into her family like a mole. This proved to be her downfall.

As she sat smoking in the kitchen she recalled a simple gesture William had made on their wedding night which she'd thought profound and extraordinary at the time: he'd offered her an ashtray for her cigarette. Suddenly she realized he was there to care for her and she for him.

With this bitter thought she took off her second-hand wedding ring, bought at a pawnshop, and put it on her other hand, stubbed out her cigarette and went upstairs to pack her bag.

When William returned she wasn't short of words.

"I could have been in an accident. You didn't wait to find out, did you?"

"Perhaps you spent the night with someone."

"Perhaps! A likely story! And now it's six o'clock. As far as you knew I had not come back. What about the childrens' lunch? Who was to provide it?"

"Rosalinde, I knew, would do the honours."

"Rosalinde! Every one must serve you day and night while you go your own way! Just because you're a writer you think you're a cut above everyone else. Let me tell you something, you're smack in the tradition of sacred Irish literary cows. Conspicuous and untouchable, they graze off other people. Everyone must regard them with awe."

"Spare me this, it doesn't become you."

"Believe me, I don't regard you with awe, you're stuffed with egotism. I will no longer feed the big white cow its holy diet. I suppose you wish me dead?" She asked, turning on him suddenly and smiling like a tiger.

"No." He replied uncertainly.

"Yes, it would suit you well. Dead and gone, out of the way, no more impediment for you and Miss Fine Romance. She's so delicate I bet she could tear up a telephone directory with her hands."

"Lay off!"

"I won't lay off. I'm sick of your cruelty and indifference. You're both like beasts of the field: honking, mating and mounting, smashing everything of value with your careless hooves."

"I like that."

"Well you can stuff it up your literary arse! If I'd been killed in an accident could you have coped with the laundry? Meals? Cleaning? Bathing? Caring?"

"I suppose so."

"Oh yes, throw out your great white paps! I doubt it very much, you haven't got any, but you'd better start developing them soon!" She shouted, slamming the front door.

Flight

The only way out of besieged Berlin was by airbus, and the following day Tess went to arrange her flight with Herb Canning, a PanAm pilot who lived across the street. She found him upstairs on his training bicycle, dressed in shorts, pedalling away.

"After fifty an airline pilot has to watch his health," he explained, rivulets of sweat pouring down his face and chest. "I have to be a hundred percent fit or I lose my job. Now let me see how far have I gone? Tess, please pass me my glasses." Peering at a dial on the handlebars, he announced "six kilometres, not bad," and swung himself off. "Let's go down." They descended to the sitting room. There were objects everywhere: anoraks, a transistor radio shaped like a football, cassettes strewn on the floor, a kite which had landed on a rubber plant in the corner and been left there askew, a pair of skates propped up against the wall, books, hi-fi, a Tiffany lamp, no expense spared and absolute bedlam. Two pampered dogs watched from a pile of clothes.

"Kath and the kids have gone to a Club Med to get some sun," he said excusing the mess with a wave of a hairy hand. "Now Tess, what can I do for you?"

"Help me get away Herb," she begged. "You know how things are. I can stand it no longer, I have to go."

"Sure, I'll be glad to help. We both think you've had a lousy time. When do you want to leave?"

"Monday," she said.

"Okay, I could take you with me to Tempelhof Monday morning. Yes, at ten to eight I'll be in my car around the corner by the supermarket. I'll get you on an early plane. Don't worry, honey, before you know where you are you'll be in Hanover. A painless exit from Berlin."

"Thank God for you, Herb."

The Hindemanns were in their kitchen. Rosalinde, expecting guests, was preparing beef stroganoff and the smell of frying onions pervaded the air.

"Could I stay with you Sunday night?" Tess asked.

Walter, checking the wine in the fridge turned round smiling. "Of course, all in the same bed, myself and two beautiful women, I can't think of anything better."

"You horrible man!" Rosalinde shrieked, "Can't you see something's wrong?" She stood at the stove with the ladle in her hand. "What's happening, Tess? You're so pale."

"I'm going Monday morning, it's all fixed, but I'd rather leave the house while the children are asleep and stay Sunday night with you."

"Of course. It's London, isn't it?"

"Yes."

"What will you do there?"

"I don't know. Start a new life, this one's in pieces."

Two empty bottles of Niersteiner stood on the sitting room table and McDaid was slurring his words.

"You always tell me you're leaving," he said, baring his teeth and pulling the cork of a third. Leaning back on the couch he scrutinized her with puckered brows, eyes narrowed, stroking his beard. "Your hands," he growled, "are getting old. Time to wear gloves."

Tess had been drinking too, but her head was clear. The sourness of your bones, she thought, dries me out. The grandfather clocks, anxious with the time, struck eleven, one ahead of the other.

Her eyes fell on a poster she had fixed to the wall, the first photograph of the world, biblical paradise, taken from the moon where nothing grew. And what were they doing in this paradise? Savaging each other like demons. Speechless, she left the room.

Holding the gilt frame of the hall mirror she peered into the glass, gazing beyond her own reflection to a memory of herself aged six. She stood on the road before the Presbyterian manse in Peddie. A team of oxen waited patiently, stamping and switching the flies away — all haunch, with dried dung beneath their tails. In the hooded ox-wagon the Reverend Patterson was taking his family to the sea for Christmas. Then her brother arrived and, suitcase in hand, bent down to give her a kiss. "Be good, Sis," he said, as he sprang onto the back. A flap of canvas was drawn aside as hands reached out to help him in. She shifted slightly, feeling the pain of departure. Leaping up into the driving seat, the Xhosa driver arranged his coat with ceremony and gave a cry, cracking his whip in the air. A piccanniny led the team by a halter as the dust rose and they slowly rocked away. She stood barefoot and alone. A hen — a white blur — pecked on the road beside her while a cloud of dust grew out of the hill. She had never forgotten the pain of being abandoned she had felt then. Now she was about to inflict it upon her own children.

She went up to the nursery and kissed her sleeping sons with a keen sense of betrayal. Nicolas was coughing in his sleep. From the corner of the room came the sound of the hamster moving in his box, nibbling the sleeve of a shirt thrown across it. She picked it up and noticed the cuff was in shreds. Who would mend that?

Rapidly now, she went into her bedroom and from under the bed pulled a suitcase already labelled 'Tessa McDaid, London', she slipped on her coat, and let herself quietly out of the front door. Beskinstrasse was sparkling in the snow, the street lamps lighting up silence.

William stood at the window watching her cross the frozen street to the Hindemann's house and thought: What have I done? What in the world have I done? But he did not move.

Walter opened the door. "Tess, you at last. Rosalinde and I have been waiting for you with a bottle of champagne. We must celebrate this departure. You are doing the right thing, I feel it in my bones." Then, more grandly, "I would have thee gone for thy sake. But stay," he held her at arm's length, "there upon thy cheek the stain doth sit of an old tear that is not washed off yet." He was given to the Shakespearian at times.

"An old tear," she smiled, "Do me a favour and kiss it away."

Rosalinde was hunched up in her chair moaning.

"I've had such a shock today", she said, "from my awful old mother. You cannot guess what she told me, it's terrible, after all this time the truth comes out. I am ashamed. Can you guess how she met my father? No, I cannot tell you it is such a disgrace. Well, through an advertisement."

"Advertisement?"

"Yes," she sighed. "She advertised for a husband, those are my origins, my mother had to advertise for a husband, in the newspaper!" Angrily she picked up the *Tagesspiegel* and slapped it down on the table. "And he responded, imagine that? I cannot get drunk enough." She looked down into the bottom of the glass and hissed "*Scheisse!*"

Walter's skin was aflame with alcohol. His mind should have warned his body it was time to slow down but it hadn't. Tess frequently saw him from her window returning from the Bierkeller on his bicycle after hours, gliding past, cut off from the waist down, a bag full of bottles swaying from the handlebars.

"We will have a bath and breakfast ready for you in good time tomorrow," he said. "Eight o'clock, is that right? Never fear, your friends will look after you."

Next morning, true to his word, Herb waited beside the supermarket. When she came round the corner he was clearing the ice off the car windows. Clouds of fumes came from the exhaust.

When they reached Tempelhof airport he not only took her suitcase, he held her hand. Everyone knew him, they smiled at checkpoints, opened the gates. When she reached the top of the steps she looked down and there he was below smiling, waving thumbs up — Godspeed, have courage, don't look back.

The moment you act you are supported, she thought, looking past the wing of the plane and watching the city recede. Accept defeat and you stand alone. Why had no one told her?

*H*anover

Tessa stood on the steps of Hanover Station with two hours to kill until the train left. A light fall of snow drifted across the square on the far side of which stood a large department store. She decided to go in there to escape the cold, and once inside, began to ride the escalators. Undisturbed, she could observe the place, and the movement gave her an irrational sense of being delivered.

The store was celebrating the approaching new year. Shop assistants smiled, cash registers sang, masks grimaced, streamers whirled in the circulation of hot air and on the distant windows snow was blown against the panes, the white paws of winter.

That she had deserted her children was a thought difficult to bear, but once set upon a course of action she would carry it through, however badly. She felt her mouth move. Was she thinking aloud?

Presently she found herself in the Mens' Department. There a brown cashmere sweater was draped on a stand, a soft rich-looking garment. She could see it on William: if only she had the money. Then it struck her — nevermore. It brought back to mind *Robinson Crusoe*, the film she had seen with the children, where he'd been faced with the figure in the field, the empty gown filled by the wind, invoking memories so strong that it seemed for a moment all resolution might waver.

She felt there was no escape, she wanted to destroy the thought of William, bury him, but he would rise to haunt her even if she travelled to the ends of the earth. It seemed to her at that moment there was no one nearer to her than Robinson Crusoe and, curiously, she imagined the old man there with her on the escalator, remonstrating.

"Why bury him?" he asked loftily.

"I must," she said. "I will not be myself, you understand, until I do. I'm no good to anyone, least of all myself. I'll go on seeking revenge — torturing myself with images of them, the lovers — and suspicion, like the moan of a high wind blowing through my mind, will not cease."

"I am familiar with that," said Crusoe. "And well I know the high wind, the roar of it. Where will the vessel be struck next? How long will it hold?"

"Quite."

"The waves rough and terrible. But once cast into the

water one grasps onto anything. Why didn't you threaten suicide? You were near enough.''

"I don't know. It's not something I could use.''

"So you are stranded?''

"Yes.''

"Yet feel some hope of deliverance?''

"I have the ticket to Ostend. Here,'' she said, tapping her handbag.

"H'mm.'' He scratched his beard. "It's right to obey the secret impulse of the mind, but as you see, there's not only the present to contend with, there's the past also. When you noticed that sweater you were distressed.''

"It came upon me suddenly.''

"You did well to invoke me then, who scorns pity.'' He stuck his beard out like a dagger. "I will give you none. Why smile?''

"You're so adamant,'' she said.

"You may smile but you might thank me. Sentiment could bring you to your knees. Stand back and regard yourself with a chill eye.''

"Right, how does one find the courage?''

"That word is deceptive.'' he replied. "Courage occurs when alternatives have been eliminated. Building my fort, sowing my field, hunting, making clothes, thrown back on necessity, I managed, even thrived. Of course things are not presented as emphatically to you.''

He seemed to be fading away, dressed in skins, whirling down the escalators in his homemade shoes, but he looked back and said with a wink: "Blackbirds fatten in hard weather."

The old devil, she thought fondly as he gave a wave and was gone.

In spite of what the film had suggested he had never really been troubled by love, she thought. Humility before God was one thing, he had triumphed in many ways, but when Friday appeared he saw him at once as inferior. He needed a servant and one was mercifully provided. The footprint in the sand, when first discovered, had posed a question which was never properly answered by the heart.

Still, he had been of help, she felt stronger. Things could commence now, she thought. The pace changing, she could breathe at last. Whatever happened, it was a move in the right direction. One of the masks twirling around in the shop resembled Crusoe, and it was smiling.

Throughout Europe trains were speeding in one direction or another, voices announcing platforms, times of departure, destinations, rose to the stratosphere in one great polyglot gargle of sound as passengers scurried up and down steps laden with baggage.

On Hanover Station the voice over the loudspeaker boomed the train to Ostend would leave from platform five.

Tessa made her way there, the handle of her suitcase cutting into her hand. Finding an empty compartment she settled herself at the window. Passengers hurried past, muffled up, and porters, wheeling trolleys with hands blue from the cold, cried out in sharp urgent voices.

Across the tracks was an old steam locomotive, the drivers were stoking the engine. Pure white smoke shot from the stack, steam hissing above the wheels. Smoke and steam were held together in the icy air, and then they themselves were off.

*T*he Train to Ostend

A young man carrying a suitcase took a running jump at the train as it pulled out of Hanover Station. Whistling to himself, he went along the corridor and chose the compartment where Tess sat alone gazing out of the window. She looked round nervously and gave a rather wan smile at the sight of him, his casual and friendly appearance. He was about twenty-one, heavy horn-rimmed spectacles over deep-set eyes, a high enquiring brow topped by a widow's peak, broad nose, flesh sunken round the rather prominent full mouth, a strong square jaw. All in all rather like a white negro, she thought, attractive.

Then she turned her face to the window again, aware of a growing sense of desolation as she sped away from her family, worrying that the oven didn't register the correct temperature, that the iron wasn't thermostatically controlled. When the pipes froze in the basement, would they know to put candles underneath, manage all the complexities? She tried to picture what rooms they might be in.

Was that a smile she gave me? The young man wondered. Looks unhappy, pleasant all the same. Funny thing this travelling, the way you try to select your kind. Have I failed again? The thickness of my lenses, I know, doesn't help, that probing look. Makes some feel uneasy. . . Faces of my parents this morning, standing at the door waving goodbye, rooms like cocoons behind them. Great survivors, really, wherever they go. Quite fluent in German now. Live on my letters. The way she went through the post one morning, called back to Dad: "No letter from Ross today", looked at me and laughed. "I read them twice, and then I read between the lines," she said, kissing me on the cheek "I miss you, Ross". Yes, I stir the pool a little.

"Going to London?" he asked after a decent interval.

"Yes," she said, "And you?"

"Me too. I've been visiting my parents in West Berlin."

"I haven't been by train before," she said.

"Don't expect much, I know this journey off by heart. Flat lands, the occasional forest. Don't landscapes like this wear you out?"

She smiled.

"Yes, landscapes like this wear me out."

"I'm a student," he said, "Going back to University, and you?"

"I will look for a job as a secretary. My marriage is on the rocks" she said. "I want to start a new life, close the door behind me and throw away the key."

"I'm sorry." That explains the torn look, he thought. "You don't look very happy about it."

"No." She sighed. "There are children."

She looked at her watch. Four pm. What were they doing?

God help her, he thought.

"Well," he said, leaning forward. "I'm at the beginning of my life, and you're starting another. Let's go from there. Shake hands on it." His hand was moist and firm. There was no resisting his good humour.

"Your accent," he said, "Australia?"

"No. South Africa."

"Tell me about South Africa. Anything."

"I could tell you about the storms."

"Right."

"Thunder comes from the horizon, like a lion's roar. Forked and sheet lightning frequently at the same time. Then the rain drums down. Dramatic." She said. "Not like here. Suddenly all is calm. Sweet scents from the earth. When I was there I felt I was looking up from the bottom of the globe. Now I am in the North I feel I'm looking down. Old memories between my toes."

"I like that."

He was a film fan, he said, it was his great escape. Had she seen Chaplin's *Pawnbroker*? *The Great Dictator*? Buñuel's *Los Olvidados*? Jacques Tati's *Monsieur Hulot's Holiday*? *A Nous la Liberté*? *Citizen Kane*? Had she seen them? Did she like them?

Yes, indeed.

She has a sort of beauty, he thought, sad and lonely, a childlike quality.

"And *La Strada*, the Fellini, yes? Well, I'll be your drummer, beat my little drum and call your name, what is your name?"

"Tessa."

"I will call your name, Tessa, and you will free yourself of your chains." He was skittish. Beating an imaginary drum between his knees he shook his head about. "*Arrivate Tessa!*" he chanted, "*Arrivate Tessa!*"

"The crowd applauds a show of strength," she said, laughing. "You know, I led just such a life as yours once, in London, all my free time devoted to the cinema."

"Would we be in the mood for wine?" he asked.

"Yes, I think we would."

"Present from Mum," he said, taking out a bottle from a small bag beside him. "And here we have the corkscrew, and voilà, a glass too. Well-organized thanks to her. You first."

"I'll drink to you."

"Ross Barclay."

"To you Ross Barclay, your friends Chaplin, Tati, Buñuel, Welles, Kurosawa & Co. A Happy New Year."

Now he held the glass.

"To you Tess, to The Roxy Kilburn, The Royal Edgware Road, The Academy, Studio One, The Everyman Hampstead, may they never close. Did you see, by any chance, *The Ghost that Never Returns*?"

"No."

"A Russian film. Let me see the director was . . . Rom. A political prisoner is given a day's freedom after years of incarceration. You see him coming down this long walled path, the sky above. He doesn't know how to walk. He springs, breathes the air. A single flower grows out of the wall and he picks it, smells it. What a shot! That freedom: strange and unbearably poignant, I'll never forget it."

I am making that walk, she thought.

She said: "I once met a film maker in West Berlin. He had made a film about me although he didn't know it until we met, wasn't that strange? I thought then that I was — we are — all part-fact part-fiction."

Outside, the old battlefields of Europe slid by, white scabs of snow to the horizon.

"Sometimes I feel wholly fiction, the bedsitter, you know."

"Yes, I know."

"But there have been funny times. My last bedsit was in South Ken. Landlady by the name of Blanche who wore an eternal pale blue dressing-gown held together over her ample bosom by one safety pin. Traces of different lipsticks, different outlines round her mouth, yesterday's pouting girl, last week's Joan Crawford, you know the type. My friends and I would discuss philosophy until the early hours. One night at about two a.m. the door opened and there she stood. 'I've had enough of you and your philosophy,' she said, 'you can fuck off on Saturday.' So we did. Now I'm living in Hammersmith, but I can't say it's a step up.

"The joke was, Blanche went to bed late herself, we could hear her below trying to throttle her husband. 'Please don't!', he would call. 'Help!' And then came this awful throttling cry. Day by day he grew thinner and greyer. We abandoned philosophy and lay with our ears to the floor waiting for the final gurgle, but it never came. Where will you stay?"

She was going to a South African friend in Camberwell.

"I've always been happy in London. I don't know exactly what it is, I think it has a lot to do with architecture, symmetry. Back in South Africa I saw many films of London during the war, set my heart on it, and from the first found a kind of logicality there. But I don't know much about the English countryside."

"I had two aunts," he said. "Lived in Somerset. I spent my holidays there. They had a farmhouse on a hill. An enormous fig tree grew beside the house. I remember as a child playing alone in an old wooden cart beneath it, the figs falling down around me. My idea of heaven."

But his real dream, he confessed, was to take a train across North America from coast to coast and watch the country spin out from the back platform.

They were easy company. Easy silences.

Eventually the docks came into sight. Ostend. A fine rain falling, the smell of the sea. The passengers trooped through the customs in no time at all and up the gangplank, some stiff with travelling, some half asleep.

The ship dazzled them with its lights, the smell of tar, antiseptic. They went into the lounge on the second deck. Ross got her a gin and tonic and for a while they sat together without speaking, watching the other passengers, but she was soon weary and lay down to sleep. Then suddenly she began to shake uncontrollably. Ross saw this, was expecting it, and gently covered her with his coat. Feeling the warmth she dozed off. Once she half woke to see him watching her and realized that, in a curious way, she had become his charge. The texture of his coat, rough tweed against her cheek, smelling of him, comforted her. She smiled and closed her eyes with pleasure. It was the closest she had come to an embrace in a long time.

Purvia

It was one of those mild winter mornings when rain had softened the air and the clouds were flying. The morning sun bounced off the water, hit the domes, turrets and bridges of the Thames, Cleopatra's Needle, the two attendant sphinxes, the branched ornate street lamps and griffins of Westminster. It shone in Tessa's eyes as she passed over Westminster Bridge, so that she had to squint through the taxi window for one last glimpse of the river before gaining the South Bank. She felt jubilant, as if she were coming home.

The antique doorknocker of 46 Camberwell Grove had recently been polished.

"Is this the Krupka's house?" she enquired.

The girl who answered the door assured her it was.

"I'm Christine, the au pair," she said. "Mrs Krupka's

up in her bedroom on the second floor. Follow me."

Alone in a commodious double bed Purvia, dressed in a Victorian nightgown, purred over her presents. It was her birthday. The room was carpeted in beige, white venetian blinds sliced the light, a pine-panelled unit ran the length of one wall. An antique Victorian shaving stand stood beside the window with its glass tilted up.

"My God, Tess! For heaven's sake what brings you from Berlin?" Her birds' eyes were wide.

"I'm carrying this sack of woes." Tess said, sitting down heavily and bursting into tears.

"Take your coat off, my old friend, come into bed and tell me all."

Purvia had an exposed face, pale blue protuberant eyes, almost lashless, a round high brow, dollop of a nose and a puckish mouth suited to frisky monologue. She was quick to smile, quick also to lapse into extreme gravity as the mood demanded. She had the charm and response of a coquette, and prided herself on matters of the heart. Now she listened with rapt attention, observing that her friend was once again dressed in old clothes, that her hair had not been styled in a long time.

"I see you've put your ring on the other hand," she said. "But I wonder, is this affair that serious for William? Of course you're jealous, your love is true. He, on the other hand, has always been monstrously unfaithful. But how could you leave the children with him? As much as he loves them he's so helpless, they need you. I've seen him use a teabag six times." She laughed. "Serves him right, the old sod. Of course, I'm fond of him, but I don't blame you for leaving. You've given him everything and for what? What happens after Berlin? No prospects, no home to go to, nothing on your plate. He uses you, thrives at your expense, you're his housekeeper, his wet nurse!"

With this Purvia threw the paper wrappings into the air. "The rogues of this world are a constant factor," she cried. "We mustn't accept these roles; give birth and be damned at the same instant to the domestic dungheap, the sepia background. No. But the Victorian age is alas still with us, with me too." She said, fingering her nightgown.

"Something else troubles me," said Tess. "I come to realize that I love William more than I do the children. It's a shock to me, but there it is. I look into their loving, trusting eyes knowing that I am the arch betrayer."

"I don't believe that, not for a moment. You need time to think, and what better place than here with me, your old friend who cares?" She wanted to know what William's girlfriend was like, how young. As Tess described her she had a curious feeling that Purvia was comparing herself to Anneliese.

"You've got so thin." Tess said, stroking her friend's shoulder. "Pale around the eyes, too."

"Forty-one today!" Purvia said. " 'Dust and ashes are all that remain.' " She was quoting a maudlin Afrikaans poet they both loathed, and then as quickly flashed out with Beckett: "Nothing but the sour cud, the iron stool from here on," and flounced out of bed.

Had Tess taken note of the house, she asked as she

dressed, did she like it? "You can't imagine the thought I've put into this place: a light over the bathroom mirror, heated towel rails, two sinks in the kitchen, work tables, spotlights. Oh! the details! Let's go down. There's bubbly for breakfast."

They sat in the kitchen on high stools in the sun, sipping champagne and watching the bubbles rise.

"You can stay as long as you like," Purvia said. "You and I are closer than sisters. Incredible to have known you all my life. Outwardly changing but ever the same, darling. I remember you at seven as if it was yesterday, how you looked then, walking down the path, what you wore."

"Go on, what?"

"White organdie printed with pale yellow flowers, you looked like a daisy," said Purvia. "And remember the drawing expedition we took to Buffalo River on our bicycles? Old Dog Terry panting beside us all the way."

"Yes, and the smells," Tess said. "The quietness, the sound of birds, and water filling those yellow pools."

"The heat of the stones and in the tangled river trees, those two owls looking on. What did you call them?"

"Kunath and Pickering," said Tess, laughing.

"Those were the days," Purvia said, "Just you and me, Terry, Kunath and Pickering. How complex life has become."

The house, it seemed, had been designed around Purvia's pottery, African baskets and books. In the kitchen spaghetti, grains and herbs were fixed in glass jars. She was a resourceful cook. When she came upon some rare vegetable or fish she knew how to prepare it. In matters of cuisine she was guided by Elizabeth David. In matters of the heart: Byron, Keats, Shakespeare and Browning. And as for the intellect: Joyce, Beckett, Gide and Eliot, all of whom she loved to quote at the drop of a hat and at great length.

Now all her consummate taste was on display. Her music too: Couperin, Mozart, Bach and the Beethoven Quartets. Pears soap and a large seasponge lay at the side of the bath. She had reached a pinnacle, Tess thought, not without envy. Within five years, a good address — Lily Langtry had once lived across the road — her children were at the best schools, looking English, they had a weekend house in the country and she attended concerts at the Festival Hall sitting in the front stalls. Outside the front door gleamed a black Morris 1100. Totally committed to fulfilling her appetites, Purvia was talking about her latest love affair.

"He couldn't keep his hands off me," she said of someone she'd recently fancied at a party. "There's nothing like a good fuck after all."

"And Boris?" Tess enquired of her husband.

"Never here, always working. Look, it's a public holiday today and where is he, I ask you? At work. But I must tell you about the business dinner I had to give, some deal he was hoping to make. I prepared watercress soup, Porc Farci aux Pruneaux and Mousse à L'Orange. The table was charming; in front of each guest a small bowl of cornflowers. So pleased was I with the effect that I phoned Richard in Paris. He called me back at twelve. 'Darling,' he said, 'Did they appreciate it?' 'They were dumb, dumb and blind,' I told him, 'discussed finance all night. I doubt they had a taste bud between them. And the flowers! The flowers wilted under their acrid communal breath.' Believe me, darling, it was paralyzing."

When she talked she bowled her hoop, sometimes it ran away with her. She came round to William: "I keep all his letters." "His letters?" asked Tess incredulously. "When I was staying with you in Ireland, there he was on his knees beside my bed panting to be let in, and myself pregnant at the time. You didn't know that, did you?"

Purvia loved the dramatic ploy, leaning forward she widened her pale blue eyes.

Tess was stunned.

Seated in a box at the Opera, they observed the final act of Don Giovanni. Beside her were Purvia and Christine, both dressed in silk, and Boris looking distinguished. Don Giovanni, seated at a gilt table which stretched the length of the stage groaning with good food and wine, was confronted by the avenging ghost. What had the poet said? Retribution would come to all of them, and in this world.

*H*ammersmith

Tessa waited for Ross to get in touch with her, but he didn't. After a few days had passed she called his number.

"I was hoping you'd ring," he said, "there's a good Renoir film on at the Academy."

Even if there was no God, she felt there had always been angels. The journey from Hanover to London would have been insupportable without him, his solicitude, lively company and, what was more, a friendliness untainted by sexual innuendo. He made no claims. She felt she must respond, certain moves were clear, she would sleep with him as a token of gratitude. She was free to act at last, they were both free agents and the time was right.

This prospect so stirred her that by the time she reached Tottenham Court Road Tube Station there was an ache in her loins, compelling as gravity.

"You're very silent," he said. Her concentration was poor, to say the least, she found erotic intent in the most ordinary scenes. She imagined them making love in the aisle: before everyone's astonished gaze they consumed each other with passion, brought down the proscenium curtains.

Ross, unaware of this, calmly watched the screen.

She looked at him out of the corner of her eye, thought of the way he had walked down Oxford Street, his bouncing stride, his old coat catching the wind. He was all innocence. She would go carefully, give him a night to remember. Would the film never end?

"Would you like to come back to my place?" he asked uncertainly outside the cinema.

"Oh yes, please."

"It might be awkward, the landlady lives downstairs."

"Never mind, we'll tiptoe." Nothing in the world would stop her.

"Hammersmith," he sighed. "Wish I could take you somewhere better."

She had to smile when she saw his room; the type shamelessly advertised in the Evening News as "attractive bedsitter: all mod. cons." The window looked into a well, an Ascot heater was attached to the wall over an old washbasin. On the floor was a threadbare carpet. Beside the gas heater with its damaged ceramic cylinders, which he now lit, stood an old iron gas ring, the simplest type, on three stumpy legs. The table in the centre of the room was covered in papers, the bed in the corner overhung by a light with a rudimentary glass shade. Devoid of all poetry but not of echoes, for it was in just such a room that she had spent her first night with William. Gazing down at him from the top of the stairs she had thought how he came like a lamb to the slaughter, but in no time at all she had so loved him she'd keep awake in order to watch him sleep, kiss his closed and peaceful eyes. But the past would not stop her, she could isolate that. When she said she would close the door and throw away the key she had meant it. Now she'd open another. Whatever she lost in the process her strength would be in moving on. Climb to the top of the hill and the new prospect lay before you. She'd keep her luggage light.

Purvia, on the other hand, was weighed down by the past, in a sense static, things stayed where they fell — a child's glove would stitch itself onto the couch where it was cast, her mother, always twenty-six, laughed from a photograph on the bookcase, her father, dressed in army uniform, one immaculate knee strained over the other, gazed down from the lid of the piano through steel-rimmed spectacles. When she made love, her parents were ranged round her bed together with the nuns from the convent school. They were kept busy.

She wouldn't have the room different, she told Ross, it was perfect in its way down to the last details, the kind of room she remembered.

"I'm so glad you feel that way." he said, "I was rather loath to ask you back."

"I'll jolly it up," she said, taking off her Indian silk scarf and draping it over the lampshade. The light penetrated the pink and crimson dyes with mysterious effect, casting a hot gossamer light about the room which brought a flush to her pale winter skin. This excited him.

"Is that better?" she asked, taking off her coat.

"Beautiful, the mystical East has come to Hammersmith at last. Now, Tess, what would you like?"

"A hug," she said simply, holding out her arms.

"I meant coffee or something." Smiling, he took off his glasses. Without them his eyes were fierce and strangely out of character.

"I thought you were a lamb," she said, "but I was wrong. I see you're a lion."

She had smooth lips, hot cheeks, felt strong in his arms, strong hot body, the smell of myrrh? "Lions don't tremble like this," he said, "I've dreamt of you, we got on so well, but I never thought . . . You seemed too distant, wrapped up . . . These buttons . . . too much. . ."

As he undressed her, his eyes never left her: she had a body like an athlete, small high breasts and long shapely legs.

He grinned meekly, as she slid her arms around him.

"I'm not sure. . ." he said.

"Who is?" she murmured, kissing his shoulder.

His eyes blazing, he was soon driving into her, exacting, demanding a response. Constellation of stars, a flash and it was over and he lay on his stomach with his hands under his chin, peering into the sheets.

"What does it all mean?" he asked.

"The first time?"

"Yes, I've never been able to make the transition from polite conversation. It happens in easy parenthesis in a play, for instance 'They embrace each other with passion', but I never made it."

"I hope it was nice."

"Nice? Hell, it was marvellous. And you?"

"You purge me," she said. "You're beautiful, you know." She stroked his back, her ageing hands against his perfect skin. "The blessed should not care what angle they are regarded from, having nothing to hide." Tracing his muscles with the tips of her fingers, his spine, up around the scapula, the neck, into and around the ear. "You'll drive me mad again!" Down the arm to the backs of the hands and into the palms.

"How do you know all this?"

"I've been around a long time."

Stroking his rump, fingers searching.

"Again?"

"So soon?"

"Once more. I've waited a long time, all my life."

It wasn't once more. When he wasn't apologizing he was asking her about the meaning of things, what to look for, what to do. He felt life pointless, ridiculous, he saw it as valuable and going to waste. Sometimes he was on top of her talking at the same time. There seemed this terrible vacuum ahead, he might slip down into the void. He wanted things to happen, it was all so slow, the days ticked by, listen to the clock, what was love?

She had forgotten youth, its urgency, confusion, the terrible questions, the vital need for answers. There was so much tension in him it exhausted her. "Stop, slow down for a moment," she said. "Relax, you've nothing to worry about, all the right qualities." Smiling, she curled his blonde pubic hair round her fingers.

"What are those marks on your belly?" he asked. "That scar like a rope?"

"An Irish operation, and stretch marks from childbearing. Love in the dark now. How little we know of each other when we keep our clothes on. Bed's a turnabout."

She crossed the room and took a wallet out of her handbag saying: "I want you to know more about me, Ross."

"You must have the longest legs in the world," he said, laughing.

Bouncing back on the pillows, her brown hair about her face, breasts and shoulders bare, she extracted three photographs.

"Here are my children. This is Jonathan, he's two; Sam, eight, and here we have Nicolas, nine, in the snow."

"You're ingenuous," he said, "Bringing your family to bed with you. Pass me my glasses."

He studied the photographs silently. He didn't know how to look at them. Quite suddenly she had put a burden on him, he couldn't bear their innocent faces. He felt guilty and jealous of her other world.

"What's the matter?"

"I don't know. You love them very much."

"Yes."

"I thought you were casting things aside too easily. They remind me of fox cubs, that look of curiosity, small sharp noses and slitty eyes. Yes, a nice bunch."

"All different, of course," she said, "Nicolas has an old wisdom, Sam's a dreamer and Jonathan's busy all the time."

He put the photographs down.

"You've gone through so much, all those pregnancies, that terrible distortion of the body I can't bear to think about and yet I don't feel the difference in age between us. Look at you now, you could be twenty-two."

"You flatter me, Ross. But tell me, what shall I do about my little foxes?"

"You will see them again soon. In fact I doubt if I shall see you again. That makes me sad. What will I do?"

"Have no qualms, you'll do very well, and I have no intention of returning to Berlin."

"She lives in Wannsee." Ross said, watching the sugar cubes dissolve in his cappuccino. They were having breakfast in an Italian cafe beside the station. "Works for the American Military Mission and earns an enormous salary. You could call this number, I know she'd help you get a job if you wanted. She's like that, me old Mum."

"What will I say to her? 'I met your charming son on the train. We spent a night together?' "

He took her hand.

"More than just one." He pleaded, spectacles taming his fiery eyes. The coffee's the timepiece, when it's over she'll go, he thought sadly.

"Are you tired?"

"No, awake at last."

Circles of light, deflected from the windows of passing cars on Hammersmith Broadway, travelled around the walls of the restaurant, resting for a moment on a florid painting of Urbino, moving over to a smiling cherub in plaster relief, spinning across to the counter where the Italian proprietor, washing glasses with automatic professional skill, stared fixedly back into the street as if all life were centred there.

"The morning's like shifting sand," she said.

"Look after yourself and keep in touch. Come back soon."

He kissed her goodbye outside the Tube Station.

Tucking her thumbs under the lapels of his coat, she said gravely: "You may have lost your cherry, but never lose your wings." And was gone. Never lose my wings, he pondered as he walked slowly back, what did she mean?

Berlin Zoo

Parched and trembling, Walter Hindemann reached into the fridge for a beer. It was 10 o'clock on a Saturday morning. Hearing the crunch of a car in the street outside, he cleared the window with his hand and peered out. A yellow Volkswagen had come to a halt outside the McDaid's house. Presently a tall brunette, carrying a weekend bag emerged from the car, and as she approached the gate, the door flew open and William rushed to meet her.

"There she is! There she is again!" Walter whispered, his jealous breath clouding the glass. "What a woman!"

"You look splendid," William said, "As always."

"You think?" The girl tossed her long brown hair.

"*Ja, ja,*" he affirmed, taking her all in. He was cautious of the smile and seldom used it and as for the laugh —

never. It was the great cancellation of thought like the sneeze which they say stops the heart.

With Anneliese, however, he forgot all that.

"You're a breeze charged with daisy flowers," he said to her, his face breaking into something like joy, not joy alone, but relief also.

In the hall drawer, crumpled into balls, were William's alibis: 'Gone for a drink. Back soon,' on the windows of the conservatory, drawings by the children: in the sitting room was the poster of the world and a green rug thrown across the couch: flowers which had been arranged by Tess, now withered, drooped from a vase. Anneliese had entered once again the House of Signs, untouched. Not quite, however, as Sam, watching her minutely, made his comparisons: he was aware of her different smell, her crisp new clothes, her sudden laugh, the hair on her face. As she lifted Jonathan up in her arms he felt a disturbance in the air like the beating of wings.

"What are you listening for, Sam?" asked Anneliese. "Sam always seems to be listening for something. Now listen to *me*, today I have a present for all of you and you too, William, and tomorrow we will go to the Zoo."

Sam stood expectantly with his brothers as she mounted the stairs to the spot where he kept his chewing gum under the bannister. He panicked for a moment, thinking it might be discovered, but she had opened a voluminous bag and taken out a large red-spotted ball. Her face alight with the pleasure she would give she tossed it down into their outstretched arms, crying "Here!" This produced instant chaos, Nicolas the tallest, nabbed it easily and was gone. Jonathan wept loudly and Sam, whose reactions were slow, had his arms out still. Red in the face from embarrassment and irritation she cried: "It's for all of you, you must share it!" and raced to retrieve the ball from Nicolas and hand it to Jonathan. Sam decided to wait for his chance, snatch it away, run upstairs and keep it under his bed forever. Sounds of discord came from above.

"Have I done something wrong?" she asked William. "I thought I'd make them happy but no, they are miserable. With children I have no success."

"Presents are tricky," he said. "Never mind, they'll settle down."

"With you, *mein Lieber*, I hope for more success. Schnaps and cigars?"

"Terrific!"

As he watched her crouching down beside her bag, her lithe and youthful movements, the hair obscuring her face, her silky knees, he felt sad suddenly, aware of his own lost innocence. He would have liked to make his way back to it but had lost the path and somehow, with that, had lost the present also. He felt very old. The only love to give was absolute, and yet that absolute love would never be fixed.

"Schnaps is your only man!" he said brightly.

William was beating eggs for supper. The children sat around the table, irritable and sulky.

Sam fixed his eyes on Anneliese and thought: she sits where my mother likes to sit, on the high stool. Where *is* my mother? Why doesn't Dad say? I can pretend it's her all the way up to her neck, but her face, no, her hands, no, they fly around, so I start with the feet again. Now watch her mouth so hard I can forget everything else, sound too. Dark cave, red lips moving around pull back suddenly showing large white shining teeth, quite scary. Turn on the sound again. Only laughter.

Anneliese was highly amused at the spectacle of William in an apron, at the same time she was jealous of the attention he gave to the children. She took the apron off and tied it round herself.

"I will make a large *Bauernomelette*," she declared. "Where are the potatoes?"

"I will never have children," she confessed to William once the children were in bed. "They always behave so badly. It is no atmosphere for love. You don't need them around you all the time. People are divorcing and leaving their children every day, it's nothing new. And besides, I want you for myself."

"But there's no one to leave them with — not at the moment — no one around to divorce, the field is clear, thanks be to God."

It was clear to him that his love for Tess was exhausted, but he found the subject of the children painful, on that he was far from clear. He liked Anneliese's manner though. Decisive and strong, she would put him first, defend him against his own conscience.

"When we live together you will write wonderful things with nothing to disturb you, my love, only my embraces."

She was sitting astride his lap, her skirt up around her thighs.

"Our love is strong, nothing can stop it. Everyone sees, haven't you noticed? People look at us and they are happy. I see our flame reflected in other eyes."

"You give me oxygen," he murmured, his hands travelling up her skirt.

The next day they were at the Zoo watching the elephants shuffling about in their enclosure. With sad indifferent eyes they gazed back, their skin sagging in folds. William regarded them with particular interest, he remembered the elephants he had seen in Africa and felt a wave of pity. He wondered if these had ever known the equatorial plain, could recall the wild life — the fanfare of the herd, the long-limbed trees going down like matchwood before the charge, those burning rocks, the primeval smell of dust and excrement. Hum and buzz of insects too.

Within each elephant there should be the herd in full cry, and all that goes with it, the blinding light too, for

"Darkest Africa" proved the reverse for him. But these elephants seemed ill and shrunken with the cold, was it all so long ago that memory had shrivelled, contracted, sealed itself off, and hung in the hall of their skin like the tongue of a bell sending out, now and again, dim and faintly disturbing echoes? Not bad, he thought, taking out his jotter, and making a note.

"Is it something I said?" asked Anneliese hopefully, trying to peer into the book.

"Maybe," he said, slipping it into his pocket. "Maybe."

The little red book, he knew, tantalized her. Yes, it had its power.

She gave William's arm a squeeze as they entered the Aquarium. "Pisces is passionate," she said, "*Nicht so?*" Her touch delighted him: he coloured a little. Slippery too, he thought.

The magical light of the place had subdued the children, and he himself felt inspired.

"No one," he announced, his voice echoing in the chamber, "no one ever painted wildlife like the Egyptians. Like this, not one but a whole river of fish, layer upon layer: above that the air stacked with birds. Remember the poster we had, chaps? The hunter standing alone with a fish on his spear. Beside him a cat in the reeds with a heron in its paw." Aware that his pedantry was having little effect, he added, "overhead the gooney-bird."

"The gooney-bird, what's that?" asked Anneliese.

"An extravagance," he replied, wiping his forehead with a handkerchief. "Those were the days."

There were times she knew she would never understand his language. He made no concessions, but it was his skill and pride after all.

Behind them the giant turtles, owls of the sea, pressed their white bellies against the glass, beaked heads nodding, pleading.

"Is this like the Underworld?" asked Nicolas.

Anneliese stood with her back to a tank where a small amethyst tropical fish appeared to adorn her hair.

"It is," said William, "And Anneliese is Queen. Queen Persephone."

Sam was a hunter who had caught his fish; fish and line were both in his pocket, a silver fish pendant and chain retrieved from the garden of Beskinstrasse. He closed his hand round it.

William thought of Laura's remark of the fish as a symbol of the soul. Mute and abstract, yes — that primary peaceful shape gliding, but . . . the torment in the eye!

All of a sudden they found themselves staring into an empty tank. The placard had been removed, the rocks appeared to be made of cardboard, the walls were stained, a piece of driftwood the only authentic shape lay at an angle, crisp and dry, and the light streamed down from above. It came as a shock, the illusion had been complete and the truth was shabby indeed.

"Where are they?" asked Jonathan.

"Dead," replied Nicolas. "Dead and gone. But do you see what I see?"

"What?"

"An ant over there on the log."

Sure enough there was, and interest was restored.

The Reptile House, a high conservatory roofed in glass, was the pride of the Zoo. There the humidity was such that the tropical palms, rubber and flame trees and giant strelitzia had almost reached the ceiling. Down its length flowed a manmade stream into which visitors had thrown coins.

They stood on the high rustic bridge amongst the broad leaves, William noticing small beads of perspiration on Anneliese's face which he found most attractive. Below them, on the sand or submerged in the stream, the crocodiles and alligators lay silent and gargantuan. The eyes, which were open, were overbright, the cream coloured lower lip curled into the semblance of a smile.

"The jaws are always smaller than one remembers", observed William. "One forgets, too, how delicate and refined the claws are."

Only when the keeper made his appearance, for it was feeding time, did they stir, rising up with alacrity, snapping their jaws in the air, some missing the food entirely and fastening their monstrous teeth on each other so that the water ran with their own blood, before they subsided into lethargy again.

"The carnage in Africa is terrific," William announced with a naturalist's enthusiasm, then grasping Jonathan firmly by the hand, said: "But this open bridge is rather dangerous. Let's go!"

They crossed by the lake, past the playground to the Freeflying Birdhouse.

This place had a special significance for William and Anneliese, it had been their favourite meeting place. William's idea. Born and bred in the Irish countryside he had an affinity for birds, had spent much of his youth up a tree in Kildare listening to their song and could reproduce it fairly exactly. An owl had once followed him round a wood hooting in response to his mating call.

It was a vast hall, glass-roofed and kept at tropical heat, with a sunken walkway from which one could observe the birds at eye level, pecking amongst the plants and shrubs or drinking from the terrapin pools. At that moment they were all in flight except for a blue and fawn variety, pouty as pigeons, waddling around unconcerned. The air was charged with activity: chatter and song, the whirring of small wings and the plants swayed. Now and then there was a random flash of colour as one passed by like a bullet. Here the plants were always in bloom, throughout the year it was riotous spring.

In a separate chamber stood the flamingoes.

"Why do they eat pink food?" asked Jonathan.

"So they will keep the beautiful colour of their wings," replied Anneliese.

In the lion house William noticed Sam was missing.

"Sam!" he cried.

The lions raised their heads as his voice reverberated down the hall, vibrated on the steel cages.

"Sam!"

No answer.

"Sam!"

William went pale. A vision bolted through his mind of the child sitting astride the rustic bridge of the Reptile House, riveted by the steamy silence and the ghoulish peepshow through the leaves. Saw his foot slip on the bamboo rail, his plump body splayed out in mid-air, the diabolical whip and gnash, skirmish for the soft flesh and bone, head crunched away to pulp, clothes too.

Blood, my blood, he panicked, child I love, gone. What will I say, what will I say to Tess?

"To the Reptile House!" he shouted, running with Jonathan in his arms, Anneliese and Nicolas close behind.

As they left the birdhouse, Sam had made his way back to the half-frozen lake where, beside a hut, he had seen pleasure boats covered in snow. Melting snow fell from a branch in front of him. He waited for the next to fall before walking on, the thin ice breaking under his feet, the grass beneath green and spongy.

He climbed into a boat and sat on the wooden seat making the snow into balls. If he held them against his chest it might turn his heart cold, he thought, and tried that. He took the pendant out of his pocket and looked at it.

The ducks and swans were in uproar, cracking their wings on the shore.

He was overcome with a sense of loss. He wanted his mother back. He would use his magic.

If I look up *now* I will see her, he thought.

No. I see nothing.

If I count to twenty with my eyes closed, she'll be there. Nothing, no.

If I throw away the thing I like best in the world, my pendant, if I throw it into the lake, she'll come through the Zoo gate, make straight for me. She knows I'm here.

She'll come from the other side, smiling.

He went to the lake edge and threw the pendant as far as he could, it skimmed a little over the ice and sank out of sight.

Back in the boat Sam waited patiently for his mother to come, and when he realized that, try as he might, he could not bring her back, he curled up and wept.

*B*erkeley Square

"You've a spring in your step," said Purvia when Tess returned. "I was watching from the window. But I'll ask no questions, you secret old thing. The agency phoned, they've arranged an interview for you with, let me see, a firm called Johnson & Whitnall, 49A Berkeley Square. You've to report to a woman whose name sounds like death but who spells it D-aprostrophe-A-T-H. Miss D'Ath waits for you in Berkeley Square. You'll have to wear something appropriate, but are you serious?"

"Serious enough for a bath."

Lying up to her neck in the water Tess thought of Ross. He was a strange combination of youth and age, too old for the young and too young for the old, until she came along. She hoped things would change for him. Questions! Questions! She took up the seasponge. "What were you like?" she asked it. "Was it one or many dwelt in you? Fixed to a rock somewhere in the China Sea. Poor sponge, long after your demise here you are on Camberwell Green, symbol of the good life."

She lifted it up and squeezed it over herself like a rain cloud.

She fancied the idea of the China Sea, yes she felt as grand as the China Sea on a bright day, she decided, enveloping herself in one of Purvia's warm chocolate-coloured towels.

Downstairs in the front room Sarah, Purvia's small daughter, was building a tower from pine blocks kept in a large wicker basket. She sang softly to herself as her mother laid the table for the midday snack. This was a platter of French and Italian cheeses, salad in a Bernard Leach bowl, a long Greek loaf baked with sesame seeds, Normandy butter in a ramekin. In the middle of the table stood a lank madonna lily in a chemist's bottle. The objects, selected for their colour and texture like the food itself, were arranged by Purvia with careful, almost clinical hands on the scrubbed table. Not for nothing did she worship Cézanne, Matisse, Bonnard and the purple Italian lettuce.

"That heated towel was perfection," Tess announced as she entered the room.

"It takes a hedonist to know the importance of detail," said Purvia smiling as she placed a bowl of black olives off-centre.

As usual Purvia had gone beyond the ordinary: her concerns were material but in her passionate rejection of the commonplace she had once again surpassed the occasion itself. The meal had the aura of a sacrament and in the background the chapel choir could almost be heard. Dressed in a white cook's apron which reached to her toes she clasped her pale hands together, cocked her fragile head and asked: "Beaujolais?"

"Can I come to the end of the road with you Tess?" asked Sarah once the meal was ended. Together they walked down Camberwell Grove past Lily Langtry's house, the child avoiding the lines between the paving stones and chattering all the way. To Tess that vulnerable hand placed in hers came as a thunderbolt. It became Jonathan's hand, more persuasive than any language, tugging, pulling her back. She'd hardly thought of her children for days, now suddenly she realised how acutely she missed them, their embraces, the smell of their newly-washed hair like summer grass, angels in sleep, their fluent limbs, gentle ways. She was not complete and must include them in her plans no matter how difficult that might be. To get a good job was essential and Berkeley Square would do nicely.

Oxford Street was a concourse of shoppers, the magic of the night before had gone and the Academy Cinema looked tawdry. A vendor selling the Evening News cried

"Woman murdered in flat! Woman murdered in flat!" and as Tess passed called out "You next!" smiling and giving her a wink.

As the prices were mostly beyond her means she had to go to the cheapest store, C & A. There she found a dress which looked suitably expensive, perhaps, at a glance, in ice-blue bouclé wool edged in blue, which buttoned down the front with a narrow navy blue belt. She bought a long string of white beads and wound them twice round her neck.

Leaning against the railings of Berkeley Square opposite 49A, she summoned up Auden:

> Fish in the unruffled lakes
> Their swarming colours wear.
> Swans in the winter air
> A white perfection have,
> And the lion walks
> Through his innocent grove . . .

and, giving a sigh, went through the portals.

She was primarily a creature of response. It could be said she did not see herself at all. She understood very well the world around her, its infinite detail, but felt herself to be a shape which occupied space alone and had no feature, moving from point A to point B, not of her own volition, but in response to exterior forces. As she waited for the arrival of Miss D'Ath who might very well decide her future, she was completely absorbed by the impersonal gloom of the waiting room — its impoverished smell, the angles of the office furniture, its tables and chairs, the rigid desk beside the window — and thought abstractedly that they were like razors which could, and well might, take slivers off one's soul.

"Are you Mrs McDaid?"

Miss D'Ath, who had a military appearance, was heavily corsetted as if she were keeping sexuality at bay. She held a file tightly against her full bosom. Tess had the uncomfortable feeling the file was about her. The woman planted herself down too near for comfort, her skirt strained over her knees, smelling of some cruel soap, and said with Berkeley Square inflections:

"Now, let me take your particulaahs."

The file was in fact an empty pad. Tess felt she would like to resist anything written down there and decided not to tell the truth. She said she was recently married and had come to live in London. She had no children, she said, tried to imagine how that would be, noticed how thin the other woman's hair was, the slight moustache, her essential barrenness and felt pity.

"How is your shorthand and typing?"

"Good, I'm fast."

"I'll give you a test. Here's the pad."

It was a short business letter. Tess found her shorthand outlines were shaky, she was clearly out of practice. She sat down at the desk and read the text with difficulty. Then placed the notebook to the left of the electric machine and touch-typed the letter through to the end at speed keeping her eyes on the shorthand notebook.

She could hear the woman breathing heavily beside her and when she looked up saw to her mortification she had finished the letter with an extraordinary flourish:

QR//@ QPP (£U(JO (£ *)¾PE H/ Q T))E £(NT
9r 7¼48 d¼48pe d¼k3 qje f9w95 uw qje qd=8q9j5
6794w3or 285y 974 t3h34qo ¼4qd58d3.
wq574eq6 9297oe g3 j9w5 d9hr3h83h51
9 q2q95 7¼484 43⅜p7 295u 9j5343w5½.
7974w rq85yr7oo6k
bq523oo o5el

She was devastated.

"I'm not familiar with this machine," she said weakly.

"Indeed," retorted the woman. "What a pity, and after going to the trouble of buying a dress for the occasion."

"I beg your pardon?" Tess asked, incredulous.

"Your dress. C & A, I believe."

"How do you know?" Tess blushed.

"The evidence is heaah, staring me in the face, I could hardly avoid it. £30.00, a mere song." She said pointing with derision at the tag which still hung from the belt loop.

"You must admit this test has not been impressive." The paper shrieked as she tore it out of the typewriter, crumpled it into the wastepaper basket with her iron hands.

"That, my deah", she said swelling up in her dark clothes, "was no mistake. There can be no mistakes, it reflects your state of mind. I knew this would be the outcome. You've no confidence in yourself, something is holding you back. I think it's your husband. From the little you said I feel he is undermining you. You've married in a hurry and unwisely. You must have perfect confidence. I give you this advice because I'm concerned. I like you, I like your eyes. It's only by sacrifice that I've made my career. I'm now the Deputy Manager. Men don't understand us, my deah."

Her voice had softened, the "us" implied not only the whole ill-considered female sex, thought Tess, but perhaps the two of them hand in hand. The switch from contempt to overture astonished her. Miss D'Ath played the game of cat and mouse perfectly, she would inflict her own pain all her life and she was dangerous.

"I might consider you," said Miss D'Ath. "You will hear from me."

Tess retrieved her coat and put on her gloves very slowly, pressing each finger down to the cleft as if she were getting back her own skin.

"Don't bother," she said.

"So you had your hands on the wrong keys, my poor darling." Purvia was doubled up with mirth. "I know the sort. My Christ, you're well rid of *that* one."

"It was like the Day of Judgment," Tess said, "and I was found wanting."

"Who isn't? Forget it."

*B*oris

Tess had begun to take a more sanguine view of things. She was not downcast by her interview. On the contrary, she was working up to another with a resilience which surprised her, when a letter arrived one morning, addressed in William's hand.

Was the affair over? Did he want her back? Was life intolerable without her? She was afraid to open it. But she found it was from Nicolas.

He told her that he was better, but that Sam was coughing now. He wished her back. He was helping, he said, with the cleaning and shopping. The temperature was zero, and two days before it had been 14 degrees below freezing. They had had another turkey for New Year's dinner. Did she know that Sam had been lost in the

Zoo? His coat was torn and Rosalinde had made him a new one. He feared she was lost and he sent her all his "very love."

Things were precarious without her, life with William was a running disaster. The letter had come at the right time, she had the strength to protect those who loved her best, and she was ready to respond.

Standing at the door she read the letter over several times, relieved that Purvia was out.

Had William, who clearly could not cope, prompted the letter?

She found Boris in the dining-room under a red anglepoise lamp which craned down from the bookshelf, selecting his pipe for the day from a collection arranged in a basket. Like everyone else in the household he had become part of Purvia's design.

He smiled as Tess entered.

He was a stocky man with a large contemplative head and prematurely grey hair, a kindly face, but strangely cold blue eyes. His pedantic manner and lack of subtlety frequently made him the target of Purvia's open ridicule, but of this he was unaware: his life was plainly set out to be tackled with a ruthless logic. He was a mathematician and, like many brilliant people, surprisingly stupid at times. The impression of brute strength and daunting intellect countered by a rather high squeaking voice, as if there were a different man inside. He had once been heard to remark that the square on the hypotenuse would always be young.

"I saw you had a letter," he said.

"Yes, and I'm going back."

"Good," he said, "I'm glad to hear it. I've been thinking you might risk losing the children if you stayed away much longer. Go back, get a job there and sort yourself out. The flight is no problem, I'll lend you the money, you can pay me back later." He was shredding out tobacco from a pouch. "I understand William, but I pity you," he added, looking up. "Don't expect anything from him."

"No."

"If you came to England I know you could get a job here, that incident the other day was just unfortunate. You'd get child benefit, the schools are free, free school meals, too. No one starves here and besides, womens' problems are being taken very seriously now. You would find support. Let's look on the bright side. Earning your own money you would be at no one's mercy. As I say, I understand William more than you can imagine."

"Yes, I will come to London," Tess said. "But of course I could never achieve what you and Purvia have achieved, you're so well set up here."

"So it might appear to you," said he, filling his pipe, "but don't believe all you see. In spite of appearances this marriage doesn't work. With Purvia taste is a vice. This house is a demonstration of excess which I pay for, and I resent it. The bills are horrendous. I'm getting out, this is not what I want for myself. Yes, I will go and leave Purvia to her excesses."

His eyes narrowed, his cheeks were flushed. He spoke of money alone, not of infidelity, heaven help Purvia if he knew of hers.

"But of course there are the children," he went on, "I love them. I couldn't go far. I've my eye on a place."

"My God Boris, don't tell me these things, do I carry a plague?"

"Not necessarily, the point is I'm a man for solitude. At twenty-one I was a goatherd in the Dolomites, you know. Thinking about it now, it was the happiest time of my life. I lived alone in the mountains above a barn. It was a brilliant summer. Once a month I went down to the valley to shop, essentials, black bread, salami, then I had milk and cheese from the goats. They were amusing companions, responded to their names. Excellent company, not a word. I lacked nothing and had very little. It was there I developed this appetite for solitude which has never left me." A single thread of smoke rose from his pipe. Was he really set on solitude, Tess wondered? After all, he had identified himself so strongly with William. Was there someone in the background of whom he did not care to speak?

The Password

When Tess woke on the morning of her departure she lay for a while gazing at a picture on the wall entitled 'The Long Voyage'. It was a peaceful scene painted at the turn of the century. Two women with elaborate hairstyles reclined on the deck of a steamer, buttoned up to the chin and swathed to the toes with rugs. A portly man sat with his back to them beside the rails and in the distance, where the boards of the deck converged, the light figure of a young girl dressed in white leant away towards the bow. Each bore the ennui of the long distance traveller whose sense of time and purpose has fled.

The woman in the foreground appeared to be asleep, her companion reading. Or was she glancing over her spectacles, over her book, at the corpulent man? And was he in his turn regarding the approaching land or lusting after the girl in white, light as a feather? And she, the girl, was she watching the anchor rise and fall in the plunging bows or had she her eye on a sailor in the fo'c'sle deck?

One thing was sure, thought Tess, in the dense blue air, all backs were turned. And that woman in the foreground, asleep with her hands on her lap, wrapped up to kingdom come, her mouth fixed forever in a half-smile, was she too dreaming of one whose back was turned to one whose back was turned?

"Phone for you!" called Sarah.

"Good morning Mrs McDaid, this is Brooks Agency here. The Yugoslav Embassy require someone immediately, how do you feel about that?"

"Sounds good," said Tess, "but I'll be off the market for a while. I have to leave the country. Please keep me on your books, though."

"Jobs galore!" she sang out as Purvia came through from the kitchen in her white towelling dressing gown, bearing a tray of coffee and biscuits. She sat down and folded the dressing gown around her, her pale nun's hands peeping out of the capacious sleeves. Purvia's morning face, all shining bone and pop-eye, was hard to look upon. It was her most honest face. She appeared to have done battle with truth all night and come off badly.

"They can't wait to get their hands on you again, my darling, those terrible women, you're in great demand now that you're going," she said, putting down the tray, "I was going to bring this up to the bedroom, but let's have it here."

"You're wrong about the Agency, they're great," protested Tess. "Solicitous and protective. Same place I used in the old days. When we first came to London I remember a woman there gave me the advice that I must always carry a bag of pepper around with me. 'If your employer gets lecherous' she said 'you bring the pepper out!'"

"Pepper, my God!" exclaimed Purvia pouring out the coffee.

"Payday was Friday," Tess went on, "the queue reached down the street. Once a Rolls stopped outside the Agency and a little old woman in a flowery hat was guided in by her chauffeur. The whisper went round it was Miss Brooks. She'd hit upon a gold mine."

"Bleeding you all white, the old bag."

"At least I had Miss Brooks behind me, you didn't do so well."

"No, not in Heal's lampshade department. Bloody inferno down there, thank God that's over. Nice to be civilized what?" she purred, glancing round the room.

How long would the perfect life last? wondered Tess. Boris was weakening. She felt depressed but could say nothing. When Purvia left the room she phoned Berlin and Sam answered.

"I knew you were coming," he said joyfully.

"How's your cold?"

"Almost better, but I cough in the night. Dad, it's Mum!" he called. "It's Mum!"

"So you're coming back," it was William. "High time,

The washing machine's broken down."

She clenched her teeth.

"How've the children been?"

"Good as gold. Lots of work, though, lots of work. I need a break."

And you'll take it, she thought, you'll have your hat and coat on when I enter the house, or even sooner.

"Will you be there when I arrive?" she asked sweetly.

"Of course."

She wanted to tell him that things would be better for them both, say a silly thing like she'd made the discovery that you opened a door by turning the handle. She was walking through doors, she wanted to say, but she couldn't.

"Nicolas wants a word," he said.

"Mum!" the child's voice was breathless. "Did you get my letter?"

"Yes, it was beautiful."

"You're coming back?"

"Yes, tonight."

"Then I will have a surprise for you," he said.

Purvia, sitting in the car, watched her friend emerge from the house looking like a new woman. With the help of Boris, Tess had had her hair trimmed, bought a new coat and a soft broad-brimmed hat which she wore low over her eyes. The casual style suited her best. She needed expensive clothes to look good.

Purvia felt deprived when she thought of the drama ahead, she would like to be in on the act, which she felt she could play so much better herself. She could not, however, rival her friend's appearance.

"You're a demon in that hat," she said, "you wear it with flair."

"One article of clothing I feel strongly about. A mask, you know, a mask."

"Secrecy again. 'Still the water, deep the ground, there the devil twirls around.' Remember the old trunk?" she said as they slid down Camberwell Road. "The boxes of treasures where you kept your things wrapped in cotton wool? I would kneel and watch you bring them out one at a time: the Chinese glass hen and chickens, the ceramic colt, the minute Windsor chair, perfect in all its parts. How old were we then?"

"Seven?"

"Or thereabouts. We would hold them in our hands and sigh with pleasure, then you wrapped them up and put them back."

"Until the next time."

"Queer old stuff. What's in the plastic bag? Presents?"

"Yes, for the kids."

"And for himself?"

"A kick up the arse."

The grand buildings flicked by: County Hall, Parliament Square, the Tate Gallery, then they were on Chelsea Embankment.

"I love this place," said Tess, "I can't help it. Here we

spent our best years, you and I."

Once they had got onto the motorway for Heathrow they talked about sleep and dreams.

"You lead this double life," said Purvia, "sleep is a major performance with you. You'll be one of those old ladies who keep to their beds, later and later will you rise, then finally not at all. Dear Keats knew about sleep: 'O soft embalmer of the still midnight'" she quoted in a fervent voice, "'shutting with careful fingers and benign, our gloom-pleased eyes, embowered from the light, enshaded in forgetfulness divine.' I don't remember what he said about dreams. Had any lately?"

Tess had in fact had a strange dream where minute parachutes fell out of the sky. Something else too, small wafers, like snow.

"I was in this house by the sea," she said, "the landscape was flat with sandhills. A wafer got stuck onto the window, the size of a postage stamp, and I went up to have a closer look. Stencilled on it was a bearded warrior with a bow and arrow. The signs were threatening, so I roused the rest of the house and we gathered in a large room. There were nine of us. One man seemed to know what it meant, he had extraordinary authority. The invaders, he said, were the unborn generations attacking the death of the family."

"Blow me down! What happened next?"

"Well, this man who was a rather pedantic character, went on to say that the only way to resist this attack was to keep what we had left: our feelings towards each other, this was our strongest defence. Where there was real care and love we should show it. Then he mounted a small platform, announced the password: Good Morning Distance!"

"Good Morning Distance. Good Christ!" exclaimed Purvia. "You don't dream dreams, honey, you dream allegories. It's a bloody allegory, but it's charged with ambiguity. What do you make of it?"

"I recognize that Good Morning Distance can work both ways, backwards and forwards, but the dream certainly wasn't about romantic love."

"As I see it, the finger points towards Berlin. You've got the hat and there you face the music."

At this point a maverick driver in a shabby car raced past, cutting dangerously in front. "Hog!' shouted Purvia, thrusting two fingers into the air. "I know where you were, the low house, the sandhills. In my dreams too, I'm back on the old home ground. It *was* South Africa wasn't it?"

"Yes, it was," said Tess looking out of the car window at the water-logged fields beside the road. "Here we are with our feet in Europe and our minds in South Africa. All that funny stuff — the deep veldt, the Platteland, the Great Karroo, the milkwood tree, the butcher bird and Blikkiesdorp. Why, if you scratched a bit of skin the African dust would fall out. In spite of the politics."

Purvia laughed. "But we do agree England is divine," she said. "Come back in the summer with the boys and stay with us in the country house, I can't wait for you to see it, it's straight out of the Domesday Book. You can put your nose into the grass and plan your future from there."

Tess gave her a grateful squeeze on the knee, and they drove on in silence. Purvia's invitation had opened up the way for her return and she would take it. She'd acquired momentum and the world had shaken into place.

As the taxi came into Beskinstrasse Tess felt as if she had been away a long time and she was surprised to find everything as she'd left it. The neat order of the snow-covered street, the pastry shop on the corner, the supermarket blazing with activity, the silver birch beside the front door. All had a static, timeless quality.

Frozen into a single image, too, were the children as they spilled out of the door in excitement, and William in the centre looking cowed, as if he did not know what to expect. It was then that she realized how much she had changed herself.

"So, the prodigal mother returns!" he said, giving her an old-fashioned kiss on the cheek. "Welcome!" He had not shaved.

"You look different," he said. "As you got out of the taxi I saw you as someone else and I found you most attractive."

"Fancy that!" she said, "Charming as ever!"

"We're glad to have your beautiful Mum back, aren't we, boys?"

"Are you?" Tess looked him straight in the eye. "Why?"

"I've come to understand a woman's work is never done," he said, "and I hand it over with alacrity."

Tess sat down on the stair and took the children in her arms. William's words had little effect. She would not have to put up with him for much longer.

"We'll talk about that." She said calmly, taking off her hat before the mirror.